Wolf Christian Schröder

Five Minutes before the World Was Made

Wolf Christian Schröder

Five Minutes before the World Was Made

Novel

Translated from the German by
Dennis McCort

PalmArtPress
Berlin

Isle of America

1

Did you ever have a private detective call on you late at night? In a seedy boarding house, in Schöneberg, in the rain? And you heard a man's voice call your name from the hallway? Grissmann? Grissmann? No, there's no Grissmann here, she doesn't know a Grissmann. You're waking up the guests! so the landlady replies. And the rain pelting the window and the cries coming from room twelve, you yourself in thirteen; cries that shook you till you realized they were merely nightmares the person sleeping in that room was having.

Didn't the suspicion then arise that you could be Grissmann? And would this detective, had he been let in, not have changed your life forever?

I, however, being in fact Grissmann, lie here awake in the darkness of my room, a room flooded by an intermittent red and green light. It's the neon sign from the neighboring building: a naked woman standing in a champagne glass. The glass green, the woman red. Red–Dark. Green–Dark. Red–Dark.

And I know who's lying in room twelve: It's a school friend of mine. Who's had it rough in life, for whom nothing has worked out, and so I've promised him he can tell me all about himself. But tell me tomorrow, I said, when we have more time.

The crying of the sleeper muffled by the wall; the man's voice in the hallway speaking my name: In this second that is my universe. All that plus the faint buzz that now and then becomes audible—this buzz whenever fate is considering what is to be done with one now.

He said he was a private detective and had to see Grissmann. That there was a lot at stake.

But I have no intention of giving myself away. And yet, perhaps the seed of doing so is buried within me. I sensed no curiosity …

Yesterday I gave my lecture again. It's about collecting children's rhymes, oral traditions such as children pass along amongst themselves, often over centuries. Things that are endangered or already lost. I am a homeland researcher.

Krautmann had warned me: What'll you do if I disappear? Without me you're a zero!

Ah, I remember well that cool summer when the disappearance of my mentor began to seem imminent. The adage with which Krautmann was fond of beginning his introductory lecture for the new semester, "He who takes up the investigation of his homeland will lose it forever," had rung less cheerful that year—even the other assistants were struck by the wistfulness contained in the sentiment. Wistfulness I called it. Gesellius, my rival and friend, called it despair. He'll leave and we'll stay: academic orphans. That was my constant thought that summer. But only in Krautmann's presence: No sooner would I leave the institute than I would enjoy the cool, placid weather and forget what haunted me. As if I were a pupil or a student, I'd gad about the city, go for a swim in the river that was too cold for summer. As soon as I got outside, I no longer feared the future.

Adult education centers, churches, old people's homes—they're the ones I try to interest in my lecture, in the city at any rate. In the country I rent side rooms at inns. So, formerly a scholar, these days I'm just a traveling performer who has lost the ground from under his feet.

In the city it's the beggars and homeless who come to my lecture, and, let in by the churches and senior citizens' centers, they're allowed to warm themselves as long as I'm speaking. They look at me with astonishment when I quote old nursery rhymes that no child of today would know. For no child these days is without supervision, and it is only without supervision that this culture can flourish. It's a culture of savages.

In the country, on the other hand, it's the drunkards who spoil my life: but with bawling, with practical jokes, and that is not without interest for my research: They're always throwing tomatoes and rotten apples at me. Sometimes I fear an apple might hit me and get stuck in my back, in a place where I can't pull it out.

Yesterday it was the yawning of the big-city pastor who couldn't care less about my research. But even if it bores him, I thought, there are still thirty or forty people in the church hall, and a blond woman with two bright beautiful children in the first row. How did she wind up at my lecture? I was talking about the nursery rhymes, the ones today's children know nothing about, and giving examples—she was mumbling them after me with a smile and nudging her children, until even they were listening to me and moving their lips. And as though inspired by the effect I was having, I let myself be swept away and drawn into speaking about the dark side of this culture wherein through jingles and poems the childlike soul gives expression to its inklings of its own procreation as well as its trepidations regarding same—but then she jumped up, pounced on me and beat against my chest with these hard tiny fists: Not in front of the children!

Her punches were those of a boxer, short and painful. A man from the audience rushed towards us, grabbed the woman, picked her up and carried her like that out of the auditorium. In tears the children ran after her like baby geese.

I had finished and my listeners dispersed when the man approached me again.

Here, I said, getting out my wallet, for rescuing me.

He was a guy of my age, dressed in jeans and t-shirt, the uniform of the disenfranchised. He was as tall as me, though his hair was thicker than mine, his face pensive or angry—I couldn't tell. His chin was covered in stubble, some gray, the rest red. A city slicker, I thought, someone with lots of friends in the neighborhood yet who is not popular—yeah, someone hated and despised by his friends.

I don't want any money! the guy shouted. He slapped my hand up from underneath, causing the bill to take flight.

Don't you recognize me?

No, no, I replied quickly, no doubt you're an old friend, a schoolmate I can't quite place and whose name I've forgotten.

Neither of us knew who should pick up the bill.

Gregory, I'm Gregory!

So, now once again my schoolmate stood before me, albeit in two different guises—the way I remembered him and the way he was now, a thug.

Gregory, of course! I slapped my forehead with my hand. Of course, now I recognize you.

I had the pastor give me my earnings, a pittance, and stepped out into the night with my friend. It was raining, and we lingered in the doorway. A big, heavy man in a trench coat pushed his way between us out of the rain without saying a word. His wet coat brushed against us.

How has life been for you, Georg?

Gregory had no umbrella, so I had to make room for him under mine. He smelled of sweat and beer.

Fine, I said. And although I knew it wasn't true, I still felt I wasn't lying.

Where do you live, Georg, here in Berlin?

At the Hilton, I said finally. As long as my money held, I didn't want to do without anything. Once my reserves were used up, I'd consider what to do.

Your courage, the way you grab the future by the throat —I wish I had that! Gregory cried out.

He laughed. Earlier in life he had been a rebel. And a brawler and a brute to boot. Now his laughter sounded sad.

Silently we walked in the rain, dragging our former lives behind us like weighted tails. I hadn't a clue what to do with my rescuer.

Why don't we have a good meal in a decent restaurant, I called out into the rain-drenched night?

Now the rain fell harder, and he snuggled up to me under the umbrella.

He had read the announcement of my lecture on a poster and decided to look me up after all this time.

The wind came up and blew rain under the umbrella so that it no longer protected us. The street was deserted. It was a long walk to the Hilton.

Come, I said as we stood in front of a restaurant. I closed the umbrella, ending the oppressive closeness beneath it, and opened the door. Gregory hesitated. I motioned for him to go in. I furtively slapped my jacket with my hand and felt the money inside.

The place was fashionably decked out. I had read an article about it. Indeed, it was even possible that they had taken the photos for the article right here in this "Epicurean palace," and suddenly a saying of that philosopher came to mind.

Do you have a reservation?

No, I answered the waiter, but, as I see, there are plenty of free tables.

No one's come today, the old man replied with a mischievous smile, no one wants to eat with us on such a rainy night. Pick a table!

I chose a table in the middle and we were already seated when I recalled Epicurus' saying: that in life one should not call attention to oneself, indeed, should conceal oneself, and I changed tables, taking my seat behind a pillar. If other guests had been there, they would not have seen us.

Yes, said Gregory, he felt better here.

The waiter brought the menus. He shuffled through the room as slowly as possible. An old waiter, playing an even older one.

Order anything you like, I told him.

An exhilaration without reason came over me, and suddenly I remembered having had the same feeling once before years ago: I'd walked out into the street and there, parked at the curb, was a car, a vehicle of singular beauty. Confidence and exhilaration came over me.

At that time the car was the catalyst of my euphoria; what it was now, I had no idea.

I'm sure you could move a little faster! I barked at the waiter, who opened the menus and held them up to us with infinite lethargy.

That's the way the guests like it, he answered.

Well, we don't, I replied. And, following a sudden inspiration, I added: Who do you think we are?

The waiter's pale, almost cadaverous face reddened.

May I speak freely?

We nodded.

Two pathetic losers.

Yeah, you're right, I answered. But then we wanted to order.

I saw that the old man's remark had offended Gregory and, for moral support, I helped him to order.

Thanks. Gregory smiled, but there was something in his eyes that conveyed dread towards me.

While the waiter served us, faster now, I was wrenched out of my joie de vivre and finally reduced to doubting the objective existence of things generally. The gains of the evening were already depleted.

Want to know how I live?

Sure, why not, I heard myself ask.

It was on a sunny day in autumn, he said, during a stroll on the canal. He was walking along there watching the river boats—on this autumn day it became clear to him that all the dreams he cherished for his life would come to nothing. But here's the thing, Georg! On this beautiful September day that thought meant nothing to him.

Which canal was it, I asked him between bites.

It was in Berlin, at the Landwehr Canal.

As if to have his fun with us, the waiter was serving faster and faster now.

Knock it off.

Pardon me, said the old man, as he served the seafood course. He said sometimes he likes to joke around with the guests. That it was a bad habit, but he was too old to break it.

Every encounter in the big city, however, trivial, is a struggle. One can lose face at any time.

We're enjoying the meal, I said, and that's all we wanted. To eat well. And you should be inconspicuous, invisible at best while serving.

All three of us laughed.

What's up with my boy, what's up with my shy doe? I asked the old man as he brought the check.

I'll come by two more times and then never again, he answered.

You see, he knows his fairy tales! I cried out to Gregory. I was reminded of my research, of the Institute, of Krautmann, of his disappearance.

It was only by strength of will that I was able to recapture my good mood.

The marvelous dinner, the wine, had made us gullible, and if someone had come by and told us of a brilliant future, we would've bought into it immediately. It was as if I had infected Gregory with my *joie de vivre*.

Here—I showed him the banknotes I'd pulled from my pocket—here, not to worry, it's enough! Though for the Hilton it's no longer enough.

The waiter brought us cognac. It was on the house. The three of us had had a good time, he said, and he wasn't going to pinch pennies.

We drank to his health.

Moods, I said to Gregory. You had to listen to your moods. If one was feeling upbeat, such as I am at the moment, it would be wrong to nourish dark thoughts and thereby jeopardize the mood. And that was why he should not tell me about his life now but rather later, ideally not till tomorrow.

It was probably the fact that the boarding house in which Gregory worked as a houseboy was named "At Home" that enticed me to follow him there. It wasn't far, he said, and room thirteen was almost never occupied, so that I could spend the night there gratis. At breakfast, then, he would tell me all about himself.

But the landlady, I objected.

I'm always at her disposal. Get the picture, Georg?

How you talk! I laughed. Nobody talks that way these days!

He went silent. No doubt I had insulted him.

She's young and not homely. Many find her desirable, he said after a while. But still—to be so dependent.

The outline of a naked woman was visible in the outline of a glass of bubbly. The glass green, the woman red.

We'll be right there, said Gregory.

The sign over the entrance was lit from inside, and you could make out two things: "At Home" and, in front of that, painted over, yet easily recognizable: "Lodging House."

"You think home means health, healthy from within oneself. But that's not the case."

Gregory looked at me uncomprehendingly as he turned the key to his castle prison.

It was a quotation, I said. From Krautmann.

Did a private detective ever look you up late at night?

We took the bumpy, groaning elevator up to the fourth floor.

Gregory eyed me searchingly.

You have that same facial expression, I thought: the look of the researcher who sees and assesses everything.

It's a little seedy, said Gregory. Are you okay with it?

Good, I answered, not bad.

I'd seen worse, I thought.

We stood in a poorly lit hallway before a gray apartment door with glass insets. The panels were painted brown, yet a dim light from inside fell upon the almost darkened corridor. Gregory was about to open the door when it was suddenly torn open from inside and a young Mediterranean-looking woman blurted out something reproachful in a language unknown to me.

German, you have to tell me in German!

He turned to me and smiled. When she gets excited, she often forgets where she is. Then she starts speaking Albanian.

The two of them embraced; it was as if they were being reunited after a very long time.

The woman didn't look at me once, rather taking Gregory by the hand, her brown Albanian hand almost black in the dim light, leading him into one of the rooms and closing the door in my face. The number one was visible on the half-loosened plate above the door lintel. I was alone. In the weak light it was only now that I saw that the wallpaper in the hallway depicted a forest, and even though the trunks of the trees were as green as their foliage, still it was a forest, made up of identical trees, twins or clones, a dark forest, and me in it, as though lost. I wanted to leave, back to the Hilton. But the forest had cast its spell and held me fast.

I could hear the murmur of a woman's voice from room one, followed by silence. I didn't move. Then there was another noise, a smacking sound that grew louder and louder.

My hand was already on the apartment's door handle when my schoolmate Gregory stepped out into the hallway, face all red.

Don't leave, you promised me I could tell you about my life!

Here, he added, and showed me the bottle he held in his hand, here, Albanian schnapps, from her homeland. Come on, let's go into number thirteen. There we can drink to old times!

Like a pal he laid his arm around my shoulder and led me down the corridor, into number thirteen. I hardly recognized my schoolfriend anymore. All despondency had left him, and when he turned the light on in the room, I saw that he had grown younger, almost handsome.

Mostly it's a pain, he said, but sometimes, like now, it's a pure delight. Gregory laughed. Just now he was reminded of his wild youth, he said. Remember, Georg? I was a womanizer.

Yes, I said, I remember.

The room I was to sleep in had only a few cheap pieces of furniture. In one corner a sink with a leaky faucet, and on the walls, as in the hallway, the forest, only older, more faded, the green just barely suggested. Must be autumn, I thought.

Gregory had sat down on the bed and pointed to the chair for me to sit too. He had grabbed two drinking glasses from the shelf above the sink and poured for us both. We clinked glasses and drank.

All the other rooms were freshly papered. No doubt it just didn't pay to bother with room thirteen.

My friend laughed as he sat down on the bed. All traces of the big city, all exhaustion, seemed to have fallen away. Yet when I looked at him closely, I noticed that the effects of love were subsiding. Soon he would again be as old as I was.

Ah, Georg! How terrific I feel right now! There was no way he could tell me of his fortunes now. He was in much too good a mood for that.

Just for a moment I imagined that I was living there too, for years in number thirteen, that, along with him, I had experienced the green of the wallpaper as it yellowed, but, with another slug—the schnapps burned in my throat, the overwhelming taste of pear numbed me—I totally forgot this thought.

The schnapps I had before tasted like pears, I said, but the sip just now tasted like cherries.

Gregory began to laugh, in the way only children are permitted to in our cultural circle, but not adults, lest they fall under suspicion of intentionally offending others: That's the secret of Albanian schnapps, Georg!

He fell silent and left soon after.

On the shelf above the sink I found toothbrush and toothpaste, a tiny tube, travel size.

It rained incessantly.

So here you lie, I thought. I had turned off the light and looked at the colorful lights that played through the window.

Five minutes before the world was made
I shuffled across a potato glade
I came upon a house
From which three men looked out
One of them showed me a five-mark piece and said:
Gawk at this
I, however, took him to mean: Hawk at this …

A little girl in an orphanage had recited this rhyme to me. It went beyond that, but the note paper on which I had scribbled it was lost. It was with a laugh, as I recall, that the orphan girl rattled off the old saw, no doubt then expecting that I would reward her, perhaps by taking her with me and adopting her. When I was about to leave, she began to cry and then peed her pants. I, however, rushed off with the recorded material.

The detective's footsteps recede, I hear the front door open. Morlock or Morler. Didn't he mention this name to the Albanian woman?

2

I jumped up, threw my clothes on and ran after him.

Who do you think you are, I thought, king of the world, who already knows everything and has nothing more to learn? Also, what better remedy for melancholy than adventure?

The street was empty and glistened from the rain. The naked woman went on and off. Late cars drove by, their wipers scraping their windshields.

Hey, Morlock!

There wasn't a soul in sight.

Hey, Morler!

I called out the names by turns, louder and louder, the more my hope of reaching the bearer of these names waned. Only my voice could be heard, and the dark whir of car tires on wet roadway.

The key, I realized, you have no key. You'll have to ring the night bell, if there is a night bell at the "Home."

A fine drizzle came down on me, and as so often when things go south for me, it sprang to mind that my wife had left me. As long as this thought lasted I remained silent, but now I renewed my cries for Morlock, for Morler, though without conviction.

You know this place, I thought, this deserted street glistening in nocturnal light, these ugly houses, these gemlike cobblestones, this red and green light like ruby and emerald. Even if this place had been the scene of a crime in past or future, it could still be home as well.

Morler! Morlock!

Suddenly strong arms clasped me from behind, rendering me defenseless. I felt the breath of a smoker on the nape of my neck, reminding me of how Gregory earlier that evening had clasped the woman and carried her away.

All my money is spent! I don't have a dime!

Nearby one of the few cars hit the brakes, but no one got out and saved me. The car sped off.

Grissmann? Grissmann?

Yeah, I cried out, who wants to know?

He let go of me.

So you *were* in the boarding house! You have to come with me. Your stupidity has cost us time.

What do you want from me, Morler?

You won't get away from me again! That's why I grabbed hold of you.

Before me stood a big, heavy man. It was the same man who had pushed his way into the church hall between Gregory and me, whose wet trench coat had brushed by us.

Do you have your passport on you?

I regarded his careworn face; the streetlights played on his high, naked brow.

That's a melancholic for sure, I thought, worse than you. That's a suicide candidate, a man who wrestles with himself over the meaning of life.

Everything all right, Morler? Your name is Morler, isn't it?

He nodded. He said as a kid in school people would call after him with the name "Morlock." Instantly he would come down on anyone who called him that and force the person to call him by his right name. In those days he suffered greatly from this misnomer; today, however, he thinks back fondly on that time. We had to leave for America today, he said.

Fine, I said airily. I got out my passport and showed it to him.

Morler, however, didn't look at it, just standing there lost in thought, head bowed, shoulders drooping. That's not the way you stand when you're about to hit the road.

Even today, he said, even today he would attack anybody who addressed him with the wrong name and give him a taste of his own teeth!

I could tell, however, that he was lying, that Morler had long since given up the battle over his correct name.

Let's get going, I said. Of course, I didn't have the funds for a trip.

If we get there ahead of the others, you'll be a rich man, Morler answered.

Now he was in a hurry, linking arms with me and trying to pull me down to the street.

But first, I said, I have to go back to the "Home" and get my coat; it was cold and I was freezing.

The only thing you need is your passport, Morler hollered.

He tugged at my hand.

Let go of me! I cried out such that it resounded from the houses.

We're losing time, he yelled at me, pulling at my arm. I tried to free myself but he grabbed me with both hands. We began to wrestle.

So weak, Morlock, so weak?

I had actually gotten him into a wrestling hold, one I had seen years earlier on television and never forgotten. It was a double nelson; at the time I carefully noted its description: From behind your opponent you get both your arms up under his shoulders and, with folded hands, press his head down. He tried to free himself—in vain.

Okay, he gasped in my grip. Go back already. But you may regret it. The time it takes may cause you to lose out!

I let him loose. Breathing hard from the effort, we both just stood there at the curb.

He's weak, I thought, big and heavy but still weak. Just like the beggar Iros, whom Odysseus, having been transformed by Athena into a humpbacked homunculus, defeated with ease. A little old dude floors a giant—what a show!

Why should I come with you, Morler? And to America of all places. I only agreed to go as a joke.

At this point I was really freezing, the struggle had been a strain, and I longed for room thirteen. As dreary as it was, still it had a bed.

Slowly, gasping for air—I hadn't wrestled anyone since my school days—I began the trek back to the "Home." When I turned around again, I saw Morler standing at the curb as before: bent over, hands on his thighs. Even at this distance I could see how his chest kept rising and sinking.

The front gate was locked. I couldn't find a night bell. My phone was upstairs in the room. I was homeless.

Wouldn't you know it, I said to myself, a cold night outside a driveway gate—why not?

But Morler is standing there next to me, smiling, as though wanting to ask my forgiveness, and before I can shoo him away, he pulls an implement from his trench coat pocket, a skeleton key, and opens the gate.

You see, he proudly exclaims, a Berlin smart-lock! And still I got it open!

He said he'd explain it to me on the way upstairs.

Morler also managed to unlock the boarding house door for me, and, now that I knew what was going on, I stormed into my room, got my things together and knocked on the door of number twelve.

Gregory!

No one answered. Impatiently I opened the door.

A strange smell hit me; the air was saturated with it. It was a smell I knew, I just didn't know where from.

Gregory! I called into the darkness, wake up from your nightmares! I need to take off and tell you goodbye!

Here too the green and red. Then it occurred to me: That's the smell of love, I thought.

Someone turned on the night table lamp. Morler had stayed in the hall and was drumming on the door jamb with his fingers, whistling as he did, fast and off key.

Room twelve resembled room thirteen, only everything here was mirror-inverted and kept in better order. My friend's head peered out from under the covers, his face tired and gray.

I was having nightmares, he said, drunk with sleep, then she came to me again.

Only then did I notice the Albanian woman next to him.

Gregory, I said, feeling the urge to speak to someone about Morler's suggestion, everything's open, the future, destiny, life. So why shouldn't I go with him?

I could hear Morler's fingers drumming.

A distant relative of mine is lying on his deathbed in America. Whoever of his relatives shows up at his bedside first and finds him alive, will inherit his fortune.

But didn't you tell me you would listen to how things have gone for me?

Another time, I answered. After all, what's the past compared to the future!

And if you get there too late?

Then all is lost. Take care. And maybe, when I'm rich, you'll visit me and tell me about yourself.

The smell of love was dazing me.

Don't you know when you're being intrusive?

The landlady's voice was rough and brittle, the voice of a much older woman, though she herself was young: I could tell from her breasts, which she did not show the slightest inclination to hide from me.

Yes, I'm intruding, I answered, wishing farewell to her too and noticing how Gregory looked after me with his prisoner's gaze, and stepped out into the hallway.

I, however, was free to explore the world.

Let's go, Morler!

3

Morler is paying for our trip. I'm to reimburse him for everything if we beat the competition. I'm his last chance, and I believe he hates me for it. He only has enough money for the trip over. If things go south, I'll have to see to the return trip on my own. He frets a lot and isn't telling me everything. He told me in the taxi that he deliberately let me win the wrestling match.

He's playing the strong silent one, the hardboiled detective, but he can't keep his mouth shut and talks and talks. In between he inserts pauses and juts his chin out, as though he's kept silent the whole time, as though he hasn't just told me all kinds of things about himself, not to mention the taxi driver who's listening in. Faster, he barks at the driver, there's a big tip in it for you!

The city is blissfully empty at daybreak. What's my relative, or America, or Morler for that matter, got to do with me? I'd love to just race down the highway forever in this taxi.

You're wearing a death's head ring on your finger, says Morler to the driver, trying to impress me with his expertise. Isn't that a Mafia ring, a Turkish gangster ring? If the eyes in the skull are red, as with him, rather than black, he says turning to me, then the bearer has already killed.

I looked out the car window, up at the sky, into the dawn. Dreams I had no business having welled up in me. Pipe dreams, megalomaniacal dreams and the like: How I would win back the Institute and even Krautmann himself with my wealth; how a new, illustrious era of homeland research would dawn. Then my wife would come back to me and, by virtue of my wealth, a new kind of home and hearth would emerge …

Banana, limetta,
On the corner stands a man …

At the airport, Morler paid for the taxi, no doubt giving the driver a big tip since the latter's gratitude was profuse and he bounced out of the car like a child, ran to the trunk and opened it. Then he laughed at his mistake—we had no luggage.

Quickly, quickly, Morler cried out.

Quickly, quickly, I parroted him. Just generally I wanted to parrot him more and more often.

We'll enter by way of Canada. He knew his way around there and there'd be no problem with the visas.

And here, Morler continued, take a look: your relative.

We were standing at the security check and had time. Everywhere it's swarming with people, people who want to drag as many others as possible to death with them.

It was a faded polaroid photo he showed me: an old man laughing, behind him a huge house. The house was blurry, possibly the reason it reminded me of another house I knew.

Of course, the picture's old, I said. Grissmann was still capable of laughing.

Morler jutted his chin out and kept silent for a moment.

Yet even now his old man's laughter sometimes resounds throughout the house, interrupted by the rattling breath of the moribund.

Had he heard it himself?

Morler placed his trench coat, his suit jacket, his belt, his change and the skeleton key in the plastic bin; a security official shoved them into the scanner for screening.

No, he'd never been there, he said. He was told about it.

As he stood there with upraised hands to be frisked, I could see that he was in very good condition. Is it possible he did let me win the wrestling match intentionally?

It's the cook, Morler said, just as I finished with the security control myself; Grissmann's cook reports to me. She doesn't have much else to do, he said. Grissmann no longer takes solid food.

There was a delay in boarding the plane. I looked at the overly tired faces of the people waiting with me and saw the gray daylight, and a new wave of exhaustion came over me.

What's Grissmann's first name? I asked, startled from the first phase of sleep.

Wilhelm. Wilhelm Klaus Grissmann.

In–out, in–out,

Little Klaus just runs about.

Eh? What's that? asks Morler, not knowing what I mean.

A children's rhyme, I tell him. By the way, my middle name is also Klaus, just like the dead man.

That last remark was just to shock Morler, since, if Grissmann was dead, all was lost. But Morler just smiles.

Morler, I shout over the din of the engines when we're finally seated on the plane, don't you often think at takeoff, like me, that a new life is beginning now?

But Morler has closed his eyes, and the expression "crow's feet" occurs to me as I regard his closed eyes. Without opening them, he just wearily waves me off. I, however, have no intention of occupying myself, or pondering my uncertain future, so I concern myself with Morler.

Morler, sir, what do you do in your free time?

And when he doesn't answer, I put it differently: Hey, Morlock, pal, what do you do in your free time?

He thinks about God, he answers with closed eyes. He likes to feud with God.

I often think about suffering, I say after a while.

Later, over a light, downright shoddy breakfast served by an old stewardess, a piece of stale pastry and weak coffee—Morler became perky, asking for extra creamer and starting to brag about how he had searched for me and finally found me.

Actually I… Morler begins proudly, and, with his shrill voice, his receding hairline, his peppermint breath, is already starting to bore me.

Yes? I say. Go on, but I'm looking out the window.

Far below no longer the sea of clouds but this massive expanse of blue, etched in fine white lines.

Passengers are now permitted to use electronic devices, and an old-fashioned bell rings out, Morler's phone, and as he receives the message, his face grows ashen.

The cook? I ask. Game over?

Morler wipes the sweat from his high forehead.

No, Grissmann's still alive, he says, and, so far, no one's gotten there ahead of us.

Good, I say, all at once gripped by pity for this sweating detective who's just been scared to death. So how did you find me anyway?

You don't take life seriously, Grissmann. Even money and riches you don't take seriously.

Soon he'll be old, I thought. And when he's old, I'll be the way he is now. No longer the man standing on the corner, enticing the ladies. And suddenly this thought is very consoling.

4

He said it was only recently that he had caught wind of the dying Grissmann.

Schmar and Wese? Schmar and Wese?

What's that about? I ask impatiently as he grins at me as if everybody knew who they were. What's that about, you ask?

The detective agency? You don't know it? The senior partner summoned him personally down to the main office, he said. The young Wese was the only other one in the room, plus him, Morler, otherwise no one. You're sacked, they told him to his face. You're too old, Morlock, and good for nothing. He said he wanted to retort to Schmar that his name was not Morlock, but that Wese cut in: You've also stolen.

That was decades ago, he told them, and they pardoned him at the time. You yourself pardoned me at the time!

Even if so, Schmar supposedly replied, this time you're fired. You're too old for this line of work, besides you've stolen.

A slight anxiety arose in me as Morler told me this. Again he grinned. How easily I could be lured into an incalculable adventure by a nut case.

Go on, Morler, go on!

He said he left the office in a daze and almost bumped into a newly hired colleague in the doorway.

Careful there, the new man said to me. However, he, Morler, had sunk down into an easy chair in the anteroom, depressed by the dismissal.

Morler fell quiet, his face pensive and soft, as though he were reminiscing about his childhood.

All at once, he then continued, an animal roar exploded from the executive office, right through the padded door—one of his temper tantrums, Schmar being famous for them: You mean to tell me that *again* you've made no progress in the Grissmann case? That was the first time he had heard the name Grissmann.

For most of the night I remained awake; the noise of the engines made me overly drowsy; I nodded off. It may well be that Morler went on talking: I, however, went through a gate behind which lay my home city. I directed my steps to my parents' house, and was rich.

We had been in the air now for several hours. Again and again I fell into an uneasy sleep; again and again I woke with a start and heard Morler talking.

About how he broke into Schmar's office at night—locks being no obstacle for him. How he searched Grissmann's file and became aware of the issue of the dying man, and of the fact that the first of his relatives to come to his deathbed should be his heir …

My father, Morler went on, after the stewardess had brought him a beer, was a professor of jurisprudence.

The airplane fell into turbulence, clouds tore past the window. The bulk of the plane dropped, then righted itself.

I asked him whether he might perhaps want to tell me his whole life story.

The question offended the detective and he fell silent.

I wake with a start. Morler's face is over me. … And this Professor Krautmann—how I loathe Morler's buzzing, nasal voice—happened to be a friend of his parents, and when he recently visited them, Krautmann was there too. And, over wine, says Morler, the professor tells an old story: about a former assistant named Grissmann who had been arrested in front of a grammar school. This Grissmann, Krautmann exclaimed, slapping his thighs: There he was in front of the school gate addressing six-year-old children with a microphone, asking them about sayings and verses having to do with love! He said he had to bail Grissmann out of the local jail.

You father knows Krautmann? I ask, amazed.

It was through him that he was able to track me down, the detective answers.

But Krautmann had disappeared, without a trace, I objected. Was Morler lying to me?

How ridiculous Krautmann looked: the chrome dome, the hair jutting up steeply from his head, the red face with the red nose, the waddling gait. That's a clown for sure, I thought!

Why are you lying to me! I shout. Krautmann is a grand seigneur, a handsome man!

How I now regret getting onto an airplane with Morler!

Morler has had a lot of bad luck in his life. He has suffered a great deal and will suffer even more.

America now lies beneath us.

On the isle of America
Gorgeous girls abound hurrah
Pick me out the prettiest
Take her home and count me blest
Serve her now a cup of tea
Then nail her on my canopy

Good, I say, you've found me. And now I don't want to hear any more about genealogy, family trees, church registers.

Can I trust you? His face comes closer. Will you reward my efforts?

5

Later on I had Morler investigated. Whether out of curiosity or boredom I no longer remember. The Kurzhals Detective Agency had been recommended to me, but I opted instead for Schmar and Wese, his earlier employers, in Berlin.

The large glass building struck me as strangely familiar, as though it were not Morler, but I myself who had entered and exited here, and Morler's antipathy to his work and anxiety over its potential loss still hung in the air.

I was alone in the elevator, and during the short trip up the notion of who I had been earlier and who now went through my mind.

A young woman with a pretty, foxlike face greeted me at the reception desk and I wondered if the receptionist belonged to a secret society that existed here in the capital city: "The Nymphomaniacs." Little was known of the purpose or goals of this group; at most its name could be seen scribbled on walls or on pink flyers found in mailboxes.

Her facial expression was cold and dismissive.

Would you like the small, medium or large investigation?

Rather than answering right away, I looked into her bored face.

The large investigation.

Somebody must have been eavesdropping on us, for out of the inner office popped a towering old man, with a patch over one eye, propped up by a cane as long as a spear. It was Schmar.

The man is a giant, I thought.

The large investigation? he bellowed in a voice like a gong. Come in, come in, I think I even know you!

He smiled down at me amiably, almost subserviently, but before he could take hold of me and pull me in with him, I stepped through the padded door into his office.

So, the large investigation!

It seems the investigatee, Morler, had been a child prodigy. As the third son of a law professor he was introduced to classical music at the age of no more than four-and-a-half. The highly musical mother, disappointed by the absence of musical talent in both her elder sons, for which she held her husband's DNA responsible, dedicated all her love, all her energy to bringing her young son's gift to its highest fruition. The mother herself had originally aspired to become a concert pianist. Until he was thirteen, Morler's talent unfolded in the most promising way: He was already giving recitals at small gatherings, already being accepted as the star pupil of a famous virtuoso, when suddenly one evening his mother caught him off guard at the piano where he sat weeping. All his musicality had vanished. His fine ear became coarse, his formerly supple fingers crude and clumsy. For a while the investigatee continued to sing in the school choir, but even there every musical trace was lost …

I lowered the report and read no more that evening. Life plays with us, I thought. Morler, too, must have learned that.

6

Morler, do you know that, when you're overtired like now, this fatigue arouses the sex drive, that, even though all you really want to do is go to sleep, you get ridiculously horny?

We had landed. The officials had waved us through: Since we were carrying no baggage, we would've had nothing to declare.

I immediately regretted speaking of my sexuality, fearing he might respond by telling me about his sexual life.

Toronto, on to Toronto, I thought.

Morler stood at the car rental counter filling out forms, I a meter and a half away from him, tired and as if put on hold. Next to Morler another customer, female, was being served, next to me her child waiting patiently, a boy of about five or six, overly tired as well. Our eyes met briefly, the child then looking down again at the plastic flooring, which was made up of white and black diamonds; and, as though I, the homeland researcher, had made it up myself, I heard the child say to himself, softly yet audibly:

Banana, limetta,

On the corner stands a man ... He spoke the words in German.

But he didn't know the rest of it. The boy, as I now noticed, was wearing a snug white suit, adorned with rhinestones. That's an Elvis-suit, I thought, just the kind Elvis wore in Las Vegas, only scaled down for a five-year-old German.

Banana, limetta,

On the corner stands a man ...

Don't you know past that? I said to the Elvis-impersonator with a smile.

The boy looked up: There *is* no past that!

Sorry, no, I replied. The main thing is still to come!

Morler and the boy's mother still stood at the car-rental counter of the Toronto airport terminal; the two young women in their car-rental uniforms continued talking with their German customers.

I wanted to tell the boy what the man on the corner had it in mind to do, but thought better of it—too often in the past had such scenes gotten me into trouble! And, as though inspired by something outside me, by Mars, by higher beings, there entered my mind a suspicion that suppressed all other thoughts:

Is your name, by chance, Grissmann?

How do you know that?

Morler, move it! I shouted to my companion.

But by now Morler had car keys and vehicle papers in hand and was heading for the parking lot with the rental cars. The boy, however, had run to his mother, and as I stepped outside through the glass door, the woman turned towards me. He was pointing his finger at me.

7

You take everything too seriously, Morler! Maybe the boy was lying, maybe that wasn't his name at all. Children lie often, almost all the time …

Come on, who lies about his name! he interrupted me.

Odysseus, for example, I answered. In the mirror we now had the suburbs with their gas stations, their auto-repair garages, the burger joints, the oversized billboards. We were on the highway heading south.

Mankind will become extinct, animals, plants, everything. The earth, the solar system. The cosmos. It's a question of time.

Morler, who says this, sits at the steering wheel, and I don't want to contradict him. For he smiles as he says this and seems to draw a certain comfort from these thoughts. Maybe he's already forgotten about the boy over this distraction.

Entropy will get us all!

This seems to please him. Indeed, Morler is in agreement with the second law of thermodynamics which prophesies an end to us all.

Somewhere up ahead, on the horizon, Morler will turn off the highway in order to cross the border via side streets and country roads, as I have no visa.

Morler, why did my wife leave me?

How should I know, the detective shouts angrily taking his foot off the gas, since a police car is following close behind us—no, he passes us without stopping.

I thought you, being a detective, knew everything, I replied.

My wife left me too, says Morler. I loved her very much.

He pulls off the road to the right.

The sky is very high, American blue, fields all around. We're no longer on the highway but riding along a dirt road. Before us, on the horizon, lie the United States of America. Behind us the monstrous trail of dust we've made.

I still see Morler before me, how he gets out and tightens his jaw, as if he's made a decision. How he raises his head to scan the alfalfa field that reaches to the earth's curvature.

Morler, no one can see you, you can take a leak!

I watched Morler distance himself, at a right angle to the street, a fifty-year-old man with a bald pate and a trench coat, no one will ever regard another man that way, watched him grow smaller and smaller—when a verse occurred to me, one I had collected:

Five minutes before the world was made
I shuffled across a potato glade …

Morler! I shout through the wound-down passenger window, quite convinced that the rubber bands to which he is attached will cause him to snap right back to our vehicle.

A beautiful picture it is as he moves out there, against all obstacles, all entanglements, a picture of freedom. A pewter figure, hand-painted: detective in his trench coat, at this point already so far away that I can no longer tell if he's coming or going. Abandonment, loneliness, but he is not abandoned, for I am observing him.

A wind comes up. Were he wearing a hat, it would fly off Morler's head.

Blow, blow, little breeze
Take little Kurt's cap with ease
And him along as well, please ...

Soon Morler will be gone, I think. And an old thought pops up: that I, through the sharpest observation of an event, can control it; that I, as long as I do not lose Morler from sight for a single second, can call him back to the car at any moment.

Morler! I shout into the crystalline night of North America.

I've gotten out and mean to follow him, but then start running—Morler is so far away already.

The soil under the cloverleaf feels soft. It must've rained recently. Good runner that I am, I appreciate this kind of ground and I ran now as one should run: with pleasure and ease.

Morler is now very small, a bright point on the green; no two: the smaller his bald head, the larger his coat.

Achilles and the tortoise. Never will I catch up to Morler the tortoise.

When I turned around, our car was already far away, and just as small as Morler ahead of me.

I don't care to be rich, just to run forever.

Morlock!

He jerked to a halt.

He had loved his wife very much, he said on the way back, adding that the field had attracted him, he'd wanted to lose himself in it.

For the last few meters to the car I put my arm amiably around his shoulder.

We will inherit, I said.

He didn't answer, but rather took off helter-skelter down the bad road. Our dust trail extended to Canada though we were in the United States.

To the question as to when he had been happiest in his life, Morler answered: while crossing an alfalfa field on the American-Canadian border.

Thus, years later, the report from the detective agency.

8

We were in the state of Ohio. I had taken the wheel.

Just keep straight ahead, the detective said, looking out for a while at the well-paved, dead-straight highway, then nodding off. The solitude of the empty cross-country highway, far away from cities and their traffic, brought back to me that sense of the omnipotence of driving a car, something I hadn't felt since getting my driver's license: to be a driver, to be the master of a powerful vehicle, one that did whatever you wanted. Morler alone intruded on my freedom of thought, and I considered whether gliding over the expansive hills wouldn't be much more agreeable without him, whether I shouldn't kick him out of the car and drive on without him.

Morler is sleeping. I'm driving.

A car is parked on the shoulder. I see it from far away. A woman is standing next to it, a small can of gasoline in her hand which she is waving. She stands very straight, as small women are wont to do, but she is not small.

Perhaps because she is beautiful, I stop. Perhaps, because she is beautiful, I root around in our trunk; perhaps because she is beautiful, I find the full gas can.

Morler sleeps while I help her without saying a word, the gasoline gurgles its way into the tank and we thoughtfully size each other up. As I get into my car, she calls after me thanking me. But I know, without even casting a glance at her car, that the boy sits therein, in his Elvis-costume.

Morler, why are you sleeping instead of watching over me!

If I were to wake up now, would I not then be in the old house where I often was as a child? The one that belonged to us before it was lost.

We'll be there soon, Morler says in his sleep.

Good, I think, then I'll find out if Morler is lying to me.

The House

9

In a small South German university city upon a hill overlooking the river which is bisected not far off by an elongated island, there stands the Grissmann House.

It's a building from the 18th century, a serene structure with a façade of white and gold; in the Fall it's often not visible from the city because the fog climbs up the hill.

The house has always been privately owned. University chancellors have lived in it, professors, Protestant church officials.

Today the building is a museum. The beautiful house with its elegant rooms is a sight to see; the central theme, of course, is the downfall of a family as documented meticulously and with innumerable exhibits.

My father is the custodian of this house. He gives tours and explains the genealogy. He himself had lived there as a child, he tells the tourists, until his father, a shoemaker and a drunkard, was finally forced to sell the centuries-old family property. The house is open from 10 a.m. to 6 p.m.; weekends it's closed, unless one phones my father and arranges something with him.

I can still see my father before me, with his bald head, his cardigan, the way he opens the house of his ancestors and lets the visitors in, and me, not yet of school age, allowed to tear up the tickets, proud as punch.

In a schoolyard brawl, I had beaten a classmate who had argued that my father was merely a janitor, that a custodian was a janitor. I immediately attacked him. I won the fight, so my father was a custodian. Still, a suspicion that he was only a janitor remained.

We lived in a flat in a house across the street. Whenever we looked out the window, we had the magnificent façade in view. I'm going through the rooms in my memory: Yes, in the gray room, in the 19th century, there had been a wayward son who had lied and stolen, and probably also gotten a maidservant pregnant. They shipped him off to America, well fixed. There he disappeared.

The house, the museum. For my father these meant home; for my mother they made little difference. She always advised me not to give a damn about them, to see myself as an individual, not a link in a chain—how constantly my parents quarreled over this point—to shape my life from within myself and, if at all possible, to choose the life of a professor. They enjoyed the highest esteem in this city.

Years later, when my dissertation adviser had taken me under his wing, she was very ill. Late at night she called me to her bed and had me take the oath: Swear to me that you'll become a professor.

To this day the old custodial couple live across from the Grissmann House. My father continues to give tours to visitors. Now that the end of the primacy of the white race is inevitable, it's primarily Chinese, and a few blacks from America. My father has to speak English with them.

10

Morler had uppers on him, tiny white pellets with red crosses on them. We had to take them to keep going, he insisted. On speed the breakneck pace seemed to us even faster, yet not for a moment did we sense danger, so thoroughly did the substance safeguard us. At some point the sun went down. Into the American night we raced.

Morler spelled me at the wheel, the uppers turning him into a motormouth.

Would I share fairly with him, might I not cheat him, besides, he was too old for tracking and spying, for that reason desperately needing lots of money in order to retire. Also, he was worried about his health …

All this he lays out before me, but he speaks so cheerfully, so brashly about it, that I take it with a grain of salt and do not interrupt him.

Morler, I say, as he pulls over to a motel late that night, this Grissmann, the one we're seeing, this Grissmann is, I take it, a lowlife?

Yes. Like all Grissmanns, Morler answered.

He's tired, he's high, I think—that's why he says that.

One moment, one day, is infinitely far away from the next.

Morler only wanted to sleep for an hour or two, just crashing on a motel bed for a while, this being worth 40 bucks to him, and when he paid for the room at the check-in desk in advance, it seemed to me as though the name "Morlock" were printed on the credit card.

We collapsed onto our single beds in our clothes and fell asleep immediately. Once I was briefly awakened, by a moaning in the room next to us, and in my half-sleep I knew that this moaning could only be coming from the woman whom I had helped with gas. What, I wondered drunk with sleep, had she done with the boy? Sent him out into the corridor where he can listen in on everything, as in an old Swedish film?

The American adventure, what would it lead to?

Morler, wake up, we have to move on! We slept five hours! Can you drive? Otherwise I'll do it! Here, hot coffee!

He opened his eyes when I shook him. For quite a spell he didn't know where he was. Maybe he was going through the alfalfa field in a dream. Then he came to and insisted we hurry.

We drove south. To our left the sun was rising. It seemed to be turning into a marvelous day, perhaps a tad hot.

11

The sun was not yet high as we pulled up to the portal of the estate.

The wrought-iron gates were open. Old trees towered over the walls.

Morler had wanted to drive the last miles, and I sat in the passenger seat, looking out at the green hills, and in the ambiguous morning light it seemed to me as though we were riding through my Württembergian homeland.

Slowly Morler drove up to the open gate.

It's moving, it's closing! I cried.

And in truth the two wings were edging their way towards each other and you could almost guess the monogram that the closed gate would display. With no time to lose we sped through the ever narrowing gap. The wings closed behind us without a sound. We were saved, on the Grissmann estate.

I sat in the passenger seat, in my dark blue shirt with its button-down collar, my horse leather shoes that had seen better days, my blue pants in which I liked to travel. I still remember how overwhelmed I was by the moment, such that just then, for an instant, the present triumphed over future and past. You've arrived—I thought and felt—who cares what's to come. Here, just behind the gate, I would've liked to die.

I looked over at Morler to see if he was faring like me. But no two men are alike. Morler was now driving more slowly, his face, as though carved out of wood, now hardening more than usual—that's a clown's head for sure, I thought, but it's missing humor and sass, it's a suicide clown, a clown one would rather avoid.

High beechwood hedges stood on either side of the driveway; then these opened up and an enormous lawn lay spread out before us, embellished by little rainbows that the combined action of lawn sprinklers and sunshine had produced.

The house, Morler, just look at that house!

I pointed to the end of the lawn where a large house loomed. With its façade, its rococo trimmings, the sandstone around windows and doors, it was a perfect replica of the Grissmann House of my home city.

Quickly, Morler shouted, then stopped, show your passport!

Nimble as an ape, he jumped out of the car, ran around it, opened the passenger door and pulled me out.

In front of the stately entrance, the spitting image of the original, stood a tall man in middle age. He wore a dark suit and tie, but I saw immediately that neither one was black. The man squinted at the morning sun and yawned.

Here he is, he's here! cried the detective, but, as I approached the house, passport in hand, it was too slow for Morler: He grabbed the document from my hand and ran to the stranger. The man smiled. He seemed not to be in any hurry, exchanging a few words with Morler, and, as I walked up to him, he extended his hand to me and invited us in.

He spoke German, a good German, only it was as if he had not used the language in a long time and had to bring it back to memory.

And who might you be, I asked, after giving him my name while he checked my passport and put it in his inside pocket.

Herr Grissmann's butler. Just a joke! he laughed; he was, in fact, an attorney and a notary under American law. He laughed again. His teeth were small and regular; he had the ivories of a young man. For a moment I forgot I was in the house of a dying man and joined in his laughter.

Is he still alive, are we the first? Morler cried out. His questions resounded in the stairwell. How well I knew this effect from the other house, so similar to this one!

Can we see him?

I was embarrassed by Morler's haste.

The house is very warm, I said, to divert attention from Morler.

The dying man loves the house warm, he said, and even though he no longer leaves his room, he's still ordered that the entire house be heated. Call me Greg.

He opened a door. We should take a seat in the Blue Room, he said, he needed to quickly check my passport with the family tree. Then he would announce us.

I know this house, I know the original! I cried out.

Greg did not answer and left us alone.

The Blue Room was just the way I knew it from my home city, only without the exhibits.

As we sat, we noticed the great stillness in the house. The minutes passed.

Eh, Morler, nervous?

You won't forget me, will you? With his handkerchief he wiped the sweat from his brow.

Oh, Morler! I answered laughing.

We were silent and my life began to scroll before me, my childhood, my schooldays, everything else that had led me to where I was, chance and time. How interesting it all was! I wasn't bored waiting.

Now I could see that my response had upset Morler. He looked like an old child, a child who, being old, no longer has parents to protect him; and I have no idea what devil was riding me, for I heard myself say: Good, Morler, when I'm rich, I'll take you in and you won't have to worry about anything.

For a moment I hoped he hadn't heard that, since he didn't react, and who is it who said we must keep our promises?

In this Blue Room, I said abruptly, one of my forbears questioned the infallibility of the pope. Morler pressed his lower jaw forward, his face thereby becoming more energetic, so that you would almost believe you were sitting across from a hardboiled private detective.

Thanks, Morler said. He wouldn't forget my offer.

An older black woman came in and brought us coffee and sandwiches on a silver tray; I instantly recognized her as the cook, Morler's mole in the house.

Isn't it beautiful, Morler, I exuded between bites, to finally be at our goal?

All at once I had to think of my dying relative, and how little I really knew about him.

Morler, too, had again lapsed into melancholy: Yeah, he repeated like a parrot, it was beautiful to finally be at our goal.

A young man came into the room, younger than Greg, younger than I or the cook, and yet he radiated a calm and authority such as one often finds among experienced physicians.

I'm Richard, German-American, as you can hear.

He smiled and winked at me.

Everything in the house here had to be German-American, he said. Naturally including him, Wilhelm's doctor.

So, Wilhelm, I thought. Wilhelm is dying.

Are we the first? Morler asked.

You are the first, Richard answered smiling.

Like the lawyer before, the doctor beamed a *joie de vivre* and an attitude of fun towards the work, and I couldn't get it through my head that this was the house of a dying man; rather, I thought, it seemed as though some California girls might come bursting through the door, their tanned skin pearled over with saltwater after a swim in the ocean.

Shall we?

He gestured for us to follow him.

Wilhelm will be surprised, the doctor added.

A woman had called an hour earlier, he said, she too a relative from Germany, saying she'd be here in an hour.

He led the way, an athletic type who could've walked faster but didn't out of consideration for us. He's letting us keep pace with him, I thought, and, given to observation and comparison as I am, a propensity I can never turn off, he struck me as a beach boy on his way to the giant waves. But the beach was not on our itinerary, and he stepped onto the stone stairway, which I knew so well, and climbed up it, casually, as if no stairway in the world could ever make him short of breath …

He waited for us on the landing halfway up.

And, as the winner, how is one feeling?

Morler wanted to answer but then just threw me a glance.

I don't know, I said, how should one be feeling?

Oh, you Europeans! Richard countered and stormed up the remaining stairs.

He stood still in front of the big double doors that led to the Red Room.

Who is he?

He pointed to Morler.

A private detective, I answered.

Then he has to stay outside.

We, however, the doctor and I, entered the room without knocking.

12

Maybe it was all a big joke; soon we would all break out into liberating laughter, me last of all, though particularly loud.

It was the Red Room that I especially loved. Whenever I would enter it with my father, on one of his tours or one of his nocturnal spot-checks through the family house we had lost, I often thought: This is the room you want to live in. Even today you'll sneak back in and lie down in the big golden bed. I didn't tell my father anything about it. One thing I learned: If I mentioned the house, he got sad.

It smelled of marijuana and bedriddenness. A strange figure lay in the golden bed. The dying man lay in it, small as a child. The doctor stood bent over him.

Wilhelm, he's here.

The drapes were drawn; still, sunlight found its way in and bathed the room in a golden twilight.

Wilhelm, are you sleeping?

We listened. We heard his breathing, his rattling.

Yeah, I guess it's not much fun listening to me breathe! The dying man let out a laugh that fused most hideously with the rattling and the gasping. Then he seemed himself to get caught up listening for this sound. His face expressed curiosity, and, as if to study the sound more precisely, he laughed again.

Who are you? Who is he? What about the woman?

Just then I noticed a screen on the ceiling, one the sick man could view in comfort from his bed. There was nothing to see on it.

This is Georg Grissmann, the doctor answered.

We're all on an informal "du" basis here, the dying man said. And yet, how I sometimes miss the "Sie!"

The doctor took a cloth and wiped the death-sweat from his patient's brow. Now he gave him a drink of water from a sippy cup. The dying man drank greedily, keeping his eyes closed. His eyelids were more jaundiced than his waxen yellow hands.

That's a piece of wood, I thought.

Ah, the custodian's son! I know all of you, but none of you know me! the dying man croaked shrilly.

His mouth was a black cave.

Shall I describe my pains to you, Georg?

If it would bring him relief, I answered.

They're impossible to describe!

Again he laughed.

You must stay till it's all over!

The first part of the sentence, the main clause, he spoke loudly, the subordinate clause, however, only in a whisper, the "over" being no longer audible; I supplied it myself.

He had fallen asleep.

I would like to sleep now myself, I said. It'd been so long since I'd slept, I added, that I was already hallucinating, seeing things that weren't there or inventing stuff and adding it to reality.

A frequent symptom of sleep deprivation, the doctor replied. But don't worry, Georg. You're the first to stand at Wilhelm's deathbed, you are the heir. The room with the balcony has been prepared for the winner, for the first runner-up the servants' quarters. That's the way the dying man has arranged it, he continued. As often as I am called, I must be there on the spot, day and night.

The balconied room has always been my favorite, I answered. That or the red one.

The doctor takes me out of the room. Here's the answer to the question you didn't want to ask, the doctor said. No more than two days and the cancer will have done its work.

Morler, who had been waiting outside and doubtless also listening, had caught the last words spoken by the doctor, and, since the doctor had smiled as he spoke them, he smiled too.

I'm going to sleep, Morler.

I opened the door to the balconied room, which was right next to the death chamber.

13

When I woke up, it was already night. I didn't know where I was, but I recognized the room. This is the room with the balcony, I thought, you must be in the museum.

What time was it? I looked at my wristwatch, a very cheap knockoff I'd picked up to remind myself that I might be poor someday.

Eleven o'clock.

I'm lying in a big bed at the foot of which stands a sofa, a divan, with a dark mass upon it. Then I hear a woman weeping and connect it in my mind with the dark mass.

You're in America, I thought, and a weeping woman is lying at the foot of your bed.

But no, it was Morler, lying there on the divan and snoring.

And the weeping?

That's coming from the next room, I answered myself. It's coming from a woman in the servants' quarters. The mother house, too, as I will henceforth call it to distinguish it from this replica, has always been less than soundproof in spite of its thick walls.

Don't cry, Mommy, don't cry! a child cried out, then burst into tears himself.

Quiet, I'm trying to sleep! I wanted to shout.

The weeping was then accompanied by a knocking, and when I said "Come in," standing there in the doorway, framed by the hallway lighting, was the young doctor. He tossed me a bathrobe.

Put it on and come with me, he said softly.

Morler sat up and, clearly caught up in a bad dream, cried out: Has he revoked his will?

The doctor nodded to me and I followed him.

He said my companion was a strange bird, but that I no doubt owed him a great deal, didn't I?

Without him I would not be here, I answered.

The doctor now stood outside the death chamber.

He told me Wilhelm was having difficulty speaking at the moment, and so he himself was to tell me that Wilhelm wanted me, his heir, to drink a cup of hot chocolate, with him watching me. He said he had always enjoyed drinking hot chocolate, but that it was no longer possible as he no longer had a stomach.

I nodded that I understood.

The cook appeared in the hallway carrying a large cup and handed it to me.

Just go in, the doctor said, and put all the lights on so he can see you. He can't see well anymore.

He held the door open for me, staying in the hallway with the cook, and I went in.

It's not easy to balance something in the dark: Since I could no longer see it, the cup now struck me as being infinitely difficult. It rattled on its saucer. Next the expensive porcelain would shatter on the floor, the chocolate on the floor would puddle. With my left hand I groped for the light switch. It was actually exactly where it is in the mother house; light came on and balancing the cup became a ridiculously simple matter.

Good evening, Wilhelm, I said.

They must have aired out the room; while it was still too hot, the odors of sickness and marijuana had disappeared.

The death's head had closed its eyes, but now he opened them and looked at me. The mouth opened, a horrible black hole. In the bright, almost harsh light I could see the tongue moving around in it, gray, a parrot's tongue. Language should be coming out of it, but it couldn't find its way, and it became clear to me that I would have to do the talking, when out of the mouth came laughter.

I'm drinking your hot chocolate now, I said, as he fell silent. I had stepped closer to the gold, stately bed and now sat down on the chair upholstered in red velvet.

His eyes, enormous in their shrunken face, glommed onto me ferociously as I drank, and I was ashamed of myself under his lascivious gaze.

The hot chocolate was at once thick, tart and sweet, the hot chocolate of a very rich man. I took a second sip and, thinking it might please him, contorted my face into an expression of supreme contentment.

Tastes like in Vienna, I said, although I'd never been to Vienna.

In the area where the mother house stood, the sun was now rising.

I told him I'd never drunk a better hot chocolate, that such chocolate was a marvelous thing. I said this to him the way one speaks to a child or a little dog—perhaps because my mind had wandered and was occupying itself with death, wondering what it is and what it does with us—even while we're alive.

The light was too bright for me; the hot chocolate struck me as unbearably sweet; it hurt my throat; I wanted to set the cup down, but the dying man tugged at my pants with his hand, his eyes focussed on the cup, and so I kept drinking until it was empty.

He closed his eyes and fell asleep. Indeed, now that he was asleep, he resembled certain portraits in the mother house.

I went out. The doctor had been standing in the hallway the whole time.

The light, he said, the light in the room had to be turned off. He opened the door, reached in and switched it off. All the days before I came he'd had to drink the hot chocolate, he said. Now he was free of the horrid sweetness.

He seemed tired; his German, his pronunciation, became worse.

He's sleeping, I said, adding, as though I were already master of the house, now let's all go to sleep.

He nodded, his youthful face suddenly gray from fatigue. I mentioned hearing crying coming from the servants' quarters. Who was in there, who was crying, I asked.

Oh, that, he said yawning, and held his hand before his mouth as per the old custom as he did so.

It was a woman with her son, another relative, but she had arrived an hour too late.

We said good night and went our separate ways.

Dead tired, I threw myself on the bed, and, just before sleep came, softly and quickly and with great force, I all at once felt sorry for the dying man, in his golden bed in the Red Room.

No one has ever deserved to die.

Once during the night Morler snored; once he mumbled something about dying and cried out.

14

I awoke the next morning refreshed. Through the open window—during the night I had opened it wide; the odor of the strange sleeping man was bothering me—came the song of a bird, melodic and powerful; he was defending his territory with energy to spare. The air that carried the notes in to me was cool and crystalline.

I padded over to the window, paying no mind to the sleeping Morler, and looked out onto my park. The bird began to sing again, and I spotted it on a branch of a small tree. It was a blue bird, bigger than our blackbird, dove-sized, thickset. Its tree stood in front of the kitchen, which was in the same location as the motherhouse kitchen.

The kitchen window must have been open, for the aroma of coffee was drifting up to me; it also smelled of pancakes and fried meat, all the aromas that fill the healthy man with a zest for life in the morning, so that he thinks: If I eat from all this, I'll be invulnerable.

Can't wait to dig into that, I thought, but I didn't want Morler around, so I carefully laid the bathrobe over him, found slippers under the bed and snuck out of the room. I had to pass by the dying man's room, but I didn't give him a thought. Not until I had gone down the steps did it occur to me that he had perhaps been a brutal fellow in life. Thus do poor people think: that it's only through brutality that one can attain to riches.

In the kitchen, the table was set for breakfast for the guests. I loved this big room with the big table at which the servants in the mother house ate in earlier centuries. How much more lavish it was than the kitchen in my parents' flat opposite the mother house.

I was the first, and Edna indicated to me that I could sit wherever I liked, although the frontside of the table had been designated for me, that being where the master always sat.

Then I shall take the seat of honor, I said.

From there I could see the tree in which the blue bird had sung, but it was gone now, its place taken by a smaller grayish-brown bird; it looked around nervously, not trusting itself to sing, but then indeed singing, short and sweet.

Edna poured me a cup of coffee, and, although the cook was present, I felt free and almighty, in a way I only otherwise feel when I'm alone.

Good, the coffee, I said, and let her give me a refill. I told her I wished the blue bird could be nearby so I could observe it more precisely.

Everything okay otherwise?

I nodded.

There was a knock on the kitchen door, and before the cook could open, I called out, astonished by my powerful, lighthearted voice: Right on, come in!

At first I could only see the boy, instantly recognizable from his Elvis suit. He remained standing in the doorway and looked at me.

You won't like me, I said, but come in anyway; they have the best cocoa here.

He just stood there, hatred and anxiety in his face, but also curiosity—and now his mother appeared, already dressed, in a floral summer print; she took her son's hand and pulled the reluctant one into the room behind her. The cook greeted them both affably, brushing the boy's hair back, thus inducing the mother to smile at the cook's affection. Clearly mother and child were dearer to the cook than I was, and, as always, it offended me that someone else was preferred to myself. I've never gotten on well with losers; either I commiserate with them or I feel sorry for them and show it in a mawkish, sentimental way.

Please, have a seat.

She gave their names, Helena Grissmann, the boy Kevin.

Not Elvis? I asked, to break the ice.

The woman remained silent.

I was Amundsen, she Scott. I had eaten my sled dogs, fed my sled dogs to my sled dogs; she had put her faith in technology, in the motorized sled, and lost.

She was given coffee, the boy hot chocolate. The same heavy aroma, familiar to me, rose from his cup. I would have to bear it until the death of the dying man. Forever will my fortune be bound up with this aroma, I thought. I struggled with revulsion.

Congratulations, the woman said and laid her hand on my left.

Congratulations, Georg, you've won!

How meticulously she was made up for the early morning, how the décolletage of her summer dress displayed her breasts! She wants to marry me, I thought.

There's a man dying in this house, she exclaimed, and you're staring at my breasts!

The boy blushed, wanting nothing to do with breasts, and I probably even blushed myself, since she laughed at me.

That was just a joke, she said, still it was on the mark. Are you married, Georg?

I was married, I answered.

Same here, she replied. She had not, however, given up her name in marriage.

You're pretty, I said, and desirable, and I'm frivolous and seducible, but get any idea of marrying me out of your head.

The boy began to cry, and she stroked his hair and spoke some consoling words, something to the effect that what I'd said wasn't meant that way, that the two of them and I could remain friends.

The sun shone through the window; the big table at which we were seated was made of a bright wood that now beamed like a second sun. In a moment, I thought, the blue bird will start singing again.

Have you seen him?

I nodded. Maybe he'll change his will when he sees you, and especially the child, who will certainly arouse sympathy.

Yes, she hoped so, the woman answered. Up to the moment of death, a bequeather could change his mind at any time.

I wanted to discuss sharing, but just then the notary and the doctor entered the kitchen.

Without a morning greeting, they sat down as far away as possible at the other end of the table. Without a word the cook set prepared plates down in front of them and brought coffee. Not a word was exchanged. They began to eat, slowly but voraciously, like the help. Every trace of American optimism had disappeared from them.

Why so gloomy? I called across the table, and once again I was struck by my own booming voice. You're sitting there like the help! Is something up with our patient?

What patient? answered the notary after a pause, without looking up. The doctor extended his empty plate to the cook for her to fill it up a second time with sausages, eggs, bacon, everything.

The dying man is doing well, he said with a full mouth, so that I barely understood him; moreover, his German seemed to me to have gotten much worse overnight.

What's up with you two? What's wrong?

This was their last breakfast here, the doctor answered in English, without looking up from his plate. This morning at ten his contract would expire.

The notary nodded. He needed one more signature from me so finally he could go home.

The two of them looked at each other and smiled. Sailing home, sailing home, they sang briefly in English.

How happy they seemed to be leaving this place!

But what happens if the will should be changed? the woman asked sitting next to me.

They made casual, dismissive gestures.

Edna could handle the dying man, and if he *should* change his will, he could be called, the notary exclaimed in a coarse voice in English. I almost thought he was drunk.

Is that right, Edna, you can handle him?

The cook nodded and filled the doctor's plate again.

No sooner was I convinced of having found a bit of peace and home in this strangely familiar house than I became aware, through the threatened departure of the notary and the doctor, of just how uncertain life was, of how I navigated it without compass or rudder.

I asked the cook if she knew of the blue bird I had heard singing in the tree in front of the kitchen window that morning.

That was the bullfinch, the doctor answered. Edna knew him only too well. He would come whenever the window was open and fly inside to pilfer things. The very breakfast sausages he was now eating, those the bullfinch would love to steal the most, even though he could scarcely carry them away in flight. He'd fly back to his tree so slowly that they had often tried to catch the creature by hand.

While talking about the bullfinch, the doctor's mood improved visibly; he stopped eating, smiled and related how he once almost caught the blue bird with the sausage in its beak. Even Greg put down his knife and fork and smiled. But to the rest of us, too, the woman, her son and myself, the picture stood vividly before us: the blue robber, escaping in the last second, the young doctor clapping his hands together to catch the bird between them.

Oh, that bullfinch! The cook laughed.

Perhaps it's only memory that can provide such a moment of unifying happiness as we had just felt. For a moment there was nothing divisive between us.

But then Morler came in, who knew nothing of theft, of the blue bird, of the attempt to catch it. Our community fell apart.

Morler stood there, squinted at the sun and said good morning. His clothes, having been slept in, were unkempt and wrinkled. He's got to be a tramp, we thought, and as Morler sat down next to me, I was a little ashamed.

For two months he had waited for death or for one of us, the notary said, getting up from the table. Now the job was done and he'd be going back to Boston, to the office. He would never forget his time here. However, someone else should perform the reading of the will. Here, he added, I still had to sign this protocol.

Indeed, new duties awaited him as well, the doctor began after a pause. His lady had broken it off with him, one day before he came here. New York, where they'd been happy for years, was now ruined for him, so he wasn't going back there but straight out to San Francisco where he would be taking up a position at a hospital. And, as happy as he was about the new beginning, he also felt a sadness over it that he would probably never see any of us again.

They all looked at me, as if awaiting a parting word from me as well; lost in thought, I had not noticed this, but Morler kicked me and I cleared my throat to gain time.

If I received the inheritance, I too would begin a new life, I said. Maybe I would stop time and continue living in this house forever with everybody sitting here.

The bullfinch came flying in through the open window, but, unused to the number of people gathered here, he shrieked in surprise and anger, turned in mid-air and disappeared.

And how about you, Edna? The doctor asked.

The black woman did not immediately answer, and a bell rang, and she and the doctor looked at each other and glanced at the kitchen clock; it was seven minutes to ten.

He's still alive, I thought.

I'll go, Richard said, you take it easy, Edna. My contract doesn't end till ten.

He walked to the door but then Helena stood in his way: Could they stay until it was over?

Certainly, if Edna had no objection.

Could he ask Wilhelm to let them in?

He moved the woman gently aside and left the room.

We've scared the bullfinch away, I said.

Helena's son had stepped to the window and was looking at the tree; I walked over to him.

Can you see it, I asked.

His white suit was starting to get dirty; some rhinestones had already fallen from the jacket.

Can you sing too?

The boy didn't answer but looked up at me. His face was strained, as though listening for something the rest of us couldn't hear. He began to hammer away at me.

While the child, with lowered head, was punching my thighs with his little fists, I saw the bullfinch on his branch and pointed out the window.

Still, the child was undeterred and continued silently punching me.

Up to now the boy had limited his punches to my thighs, and I hardly felt them; now, however, as the bullfinch outside began to sing again, the little fist pounded me in the nads, taking my breath away. I looked at his mother, as if to tell the woman to get the kid off me, but thought I saw her smile approvingly, and once again the child's fist struck me, almost causing me to lose consciousness.

Now I could see that it wasn't schadenfreude that showed on Helena's face but pride in her son who so bravely gave resistance to the injustice of the world.

In another moment I would've flung the little pest to the ground and pounded him into pulp. Just the way Donald Sutherland once handled a kid in a film.

Now I was holding the boy away from me with my outstretched arm, and he began to cry because he was missing me, his punches hitting nothing but air; then Edna brought him a hot chocolate and he let go of me.

You've practically eunuchized me, I said. I knew this word from my studies.

My testicles hurt. Greedily the boy drank the cocoa.

Just a moment earlier, we'd been happy.

A moment later the doctor came into the kitchen. He went to his place but did not sit down, rather taking his cup, which was still half full, and drinking the coffee that had grown cold.

He can speak. The woman and the child he doesn't want to see. But you, Georg, and your companion too.

I put in a good word for you, he said, anticipating Helena's questions. Still, the dying man didn't want any losers at his deathbed. It won't be long now. Edna was to give him his next injection at twelve.

Outside the limousine pulled up. It was to take the notary and the doctor to the nearest airport.

The two of them were no longer in a hurry, neither did they dawdle. They were like men who went to work in the morning, to a job they loved and of whose import they were exceedingly confident. How gladly would I have been one of them! Perhaps the notary. Then Morler could've been the doctor.

We all went out together, Morler included.

Be well! we all called to each other, shook hands, long life, lots of luck, you too, who knows, maybe we'll meet again. And good health!

How powerful parting can be! Melancholy took hold of, not only me, being anyway inclined to it, but the notary and the doctor as well. But behind all of it, behind the waving after the car, which drove off slowly and solemnly, there stood death, and that made us sad.

Finally we went back into the house. The whole time, though, the bullfinch had sat on its branch and watched our parting.

15

The departure of the doctor and the notary was followed by a period of calm. They had left us numbers we were to call at the moment of death. But Wilhelm lay there and refused to die. The black cook was now caring for him by herself and arranged things in such a way that I noticed almost nothing of the bodily vileness associated with dying. However, my visits to him were not frequent. He summoned me only every few days, and then often had nothing to say, rather letting me tell him about my life.

He knows a lot about us relatives, actually everything, but until now he's never been moved to make personal contact with even one of us.

Helena is a castaway, he says to me today, a drifter, a little like you—he laughed.

You're easy to understand today, I replied.

It's Indian summer outside. I have to drink cocoa, and, when I'm not looking at the deathbed, I look out the window into the blue sky. I try to listen carefully for the bullfinch whose song is becoming more and more repugnant to me.

Isn't she beautiful?

The most beautiful of women, as the name says, I answer.

When she was younger and, at one point, very poor, she acted in a porno film.

His hand, all scaly like a chicken foot, lays itself on mine, and in the mummy's face the eyes flair up.

Your eyes are aglow, it's for sure you've seen the film, I say. You probably have it here in this commode.

He cannot speak and nods. His mouth, this hole, I think, in this whole resides death.

Were you a bad man, Wilhelm? I ask, as though I were God or Saint Peter. Nod if you can't speak.

He laughs, rattling and gasping. Where does he find the energy?

We only go a little ways from the house, Helena, the boy and I, so that we can be right there when the time comes. Only Morler hikes further out over the landscape. What does he do there? Maybe he needs movement to counter the anxiety of coming away empty-handed.

I had wanted to send Helena and the boy away, back to Europe, but the dying man was against it: They were homeless, the cook told him, had no money and wished to stay on a while longer. The woman should be allowed to rest here, that's what Edna requested. Edna pities them. They were in such desperate need of the inheritance.

We often sit in the garden where the black cook lays the table on beautiful days. From afar you'd think you were seeing a woman with beautifully curved eyebrows sitting there, together with her husband, together with her child, and a boarder—that would be Morler.

Edna is hoping I keep her on so that, at the age of fifty-two, she doesn't have to change her situation. I've held out hope to her but promised nothing. She has, by the way, moved Morler into the Gray Room, so that he has his own quarters. But I think I know the real reason for this: If Helena has it in mind to sneak into my room at night, Morler will only be a disturbance.

During dinner on the terrace, I'd mentioned the notion that one must live in the moment, that one should look for happiness right in the niches of waiting, of transition; I had talked myself into an inspiration that had itself sprung from the moment.

The meal was over but we continued to sit in the sun. The afternoon set in, a time of day of which, ever since childhood, I've always harbored a faint dread, especially on sunny days.

Should I become rich, I asked myself, would I ever overcome my anxiety over the afternoon?

Morler had gone for a walk, all the way across the lawn, between the trees and beyond; we could no longer see him.

One more thing, the woman said and looked out over the park. She said she was a teacher and was asking this question for quasi professional reasons: How would I describe my character?

The afternoon was sapping my strength and I didn't want to answer; how easy it is to say something stupid when you're weak.

My character leaves much to be desired, I said finally, adding that, just before, over coffee, I had spoken total nonsense about the niches of happiness. I hadn't the faintest idea about such things.

No, she said, and looked me in the eye, the way she perhaps did with her pupils: She wanted me to tell about my character.

What would she say about her own? I answered.

Thus do lovebirds talk on French terraces when the sun causes the remnants of white wine in the glasses to glisten after the meal; lovebirds, but also enemies.

Kevin had run off, deep into the park.

She said she'd been in the Red Room yesterday.

She paused, considering whether to go on.

The dying man was asleep, she said, and she just gazed at him. He lay there like a dead man and she felt compelled to ask herself how much power still resided in this paltry body. Then he woke up.

She paused, and I asked her whether she now had anything important, anything life-changing, to say to me?

She said he wanted her to dance naked before him. But she didn't do it.

Far back, where the lawn transitioned to trees, Morler could now be seen, teeny-weeny. A figure half as large walked up to him, the boy. They stood next to each other for a while, then the larger figure lunged forward and stroked the smaller figure's hair. Or struck him.

I was moody and gloomy, I said, a sharp observer who tended to lose himself in the process of observing. As for the rest, my character changed after Krautmann's disappearance, so that I no longer even knew myself what it was like now.

Sure, the same reaction twice in a row, now that's certainly enough to drum up a character! the woman replied, angrily balling a fist.

She was, as she said this, deep in thought, perhaps not even listening to me, and, in spite of myself, or perhaps because rage enhanced her beauty, I had to think of the film Wilhelm kept in his commode, and of the fact that I would inherit this film and be able to view it any time I liked.

Morler strides across the lawn, coming toward us, the boy in hand, looming larger and larger.

Just in case we'd seen it—yes, he hit the kid. He said the boy had stomped a bird to death that lay on the lawn unable to fly. For that he was punished.

You don't hit children! my relative cried out. That stopped long ago, Herr Morler!

A quarrel seemed to be brewing, but the boy with his red cheek stood there smiling next to his chastiser, no longer of a mind to let go of the detective's hand.

What kind of bird was it that the child trampled to death? I asked.

It was a bullfinch, answered the detective and the boy at the same time, then laughing because they had spoken simultaneously.

You don't stomp on birds, said the boy's mother. How would you feel if Herr Morler or Herr Grissmann stomped on you? And how sad would that make me?

Edna, I called out, bring some more ice, and please join us on this beautiful day.

We sat there in silence, squinting at the Fall sun and enjoying life.

I'll take them all home with me.

Don't worry, Morler, you'll get your money's worth!

I should've kept my mouth shut: The magic was gone. Edna got up. She said she had to give the patient his injection.

Helena went into the house with the boy, Edna was tending to the dying man, Morler again set off without a word on his wandering ways. I alone remained sitting there, stirring the residual sugar at the bottom of the cup with my coffee spoon.

16

Before he died, William or Wilhelm, as he called himself as he lay dying, summoned me twice more; and I was with him even at the moment of his death, and held his hand. I had taken his hand with a certain dread, holding it until the business was over. I was surprised that you could easily let go of the hand of a dead man after his death.

My next to last visit at the deathbed took place late at night. Edna had knocked on my door to tell me that I should come quickly. During his evening injection, he had instructed her to tell me that I was to come to his bed at precisely three o'clock. But, she said, there was someone with him, and perhaps he had changed his mind and didn't wish to see anyone else.

I threw my robe on and rushed to the Red Room.

Already on the stairs I could hear clarinet music. It was "Petite Fleur," little flower, an old French ditty, sad and seductive, in which the clarinet begins darkly and softly, then spirals upwards in order to drop down again darkly and delicately.

I opened the door to the death chamber. The room lay in darkness, only a red headlamp threw a small, sharply focussed beam of light in front of the bed.

The music ended, and for just a nanosecond I saw the naked breasts, the dark pubic hair against the bright skin. Then the headlamp went out and the ceiling light came on. By now the woman had covered herself with the bathrobe and she brushed by me on her way out.

How beautiful that was, Georg! How beautiful!

So? I shout out wantonly, am I now disinherited?

And, for an answer, I hear his wheezing laughter, until he chokes and begins coughing.

Do you smell it too, Georg, he says in a low voice, again struggling to breathe. I smell of death.

Oh please, I answer, let's talk about something else.

And it becomes clear to me how immense the difference is between dying and being dead; that a dying man is still here, but a dead man not, and that a living being like me can never grasp this fact; and sympathy for Wilhelm comes over me.

He signals to me that he is unable to speak; usually I'm to go then, he being ashamed of his muteness.

Go ahead and disinherit me, if you like.

His laughter goes flat, no longer wheezing. He's a piece of wood. But even a piece of wood is there and not vanished into the nothingness. And I turn out the light and persuade myself he is asleep.

Now I lay in bed in the Gray Salon. I'd opened the windows and briefly looked out over the park. From the Gray Salon in the mother house, I would've seen an ugly building, one containing my parents' apartment. As so often when I can't sleep, I thought about sleep itself, and then about Krautmann's disappearance and how it had reduced me to the condition of a vagabond, a tramp. And how, through Morler, I was shifted into an entirely different situation; and that I now perhaps might actually not wind up renting beds from Romanian or Albanian women.

Rich, rich. I said the word to myself over and over again, now louder, now softer, now full of enthusiasm, now rather muted and desperate—but it said nothing to me, I couldn't understand what it meant.

From outside cool autumn air permeated the room, along with the cries of nocturnal birds, and my thoughts turned to sleep, since you can summon it this way, and it came.

Morler is already sitting at the breakfast table when I come into the kitchen in the morning, Morler along with the boy. They're laughing and chatting, and, even as Morler grows serious at my appearance, the boy continues telling him how long he had wished for the white suit. Finally, on his birthday, the time had come. He told how he'd put it on and it had fit and he said to Helena: Now that I have the suit, I can die in peace. He said he'd never take it off.

The boy tells this laughingly while Edna lays out my breakfast.

The two of us, however, Morler and I, inspect the suit and see that it is missing several sequins, that rhinestones have fallen off and that the leather here and there is greasy and dark.

Morler, I ask, what do you know about Wilhelm?

And it turns out that even Morler knows very little, only that the dying man is rich, that he came to be known as eccentric in his later years and, in his younger years, was considered ruthless and, in business matters, brutal.

Helena came into the room. She looked crestfallen, her serious face with its high brows exhibiting a certain nobility. Yes, I thought, yesterday you probably danced for nothing.

And while I'm offering her a chair, I suddenly remember what it was I was unable to recall last night: that being rich means leading the kind of life I was now leading, using money to reclaim what I've lost. I find this thought quite inspiring.

17

The bell rang and Edna rushed upstairs.

He wanted to see me.

Not me? Not me too? Helena asked.

What's that coming out of your mouth?

It was saliva, the dying man replied. Whenever he smelled the chocolate, and the steam rose from the cup, saliva would come automatically.

I drank and, strange to say, today I liked the taste.

What about Helena?

That's your business, Wilhelm answered. It no longer affects me.

Sure, you're a piece of wood. Do you want water? I ask, but as I hold the water glass to his black lips, with an infinitely feeble movement he turns his head aside and refuses to drink.

What am I to do with your money?

He, however, pretends to be asleep, and I stay with him a while longer.

Our rental cars were parked outside. Every day that Wilhelm didn't die, the bill for them grew relentlessly.

18

William K. Grissmann died on a gorgeous October day. He was seventy-four years old. His forebears had immigrated from Southern Germany in the early 19th century. For generations they had been poor tradesmen in America; then their luck changed and they became rich.

It wasn't until late in life that Grissmann took a serious interest in genealogy, a widespread hobby in the United States. He preferred speaking German to English and surrounded himself with people whose forebears, like his own, came from Germany. He insisted on being called "Wilhelm." He found out that he was the last of his line and liked making jokes about it. He had given thought to relocating in Germany, but the detective he sent out found only quite scattered relatives, and so he distanced himself from this plan. Still, images in the detective's report of an old house in a small city in Southern Germany so charmed him that he had the building recreated in America.

Just after moving in he became sick. He had no legal heirs.

On October twenty-third around seven o'clock, I entered the kitchen of the daughter-house. The days were now shorter than at the time of my arrival, and the sun no longer shone in the window as early. Something was different from usual: There was no smell of coffee, or bacon or pancakes. I was shivering. Being the first one there, I turned the lights on. There was no preparation for breakfast.

They've all left, I thought, I'm all alone in the house; all these days they've been putting on an act for you and now they've left you behind, without money, stranded.

Suddenly it occurred to me that part of one of Helena's incisor teeth was missing. Yesterday that had struck me as incidental,—now, in the cold, empty kitchen it took on great significance—I just didn't know precisely what.

Now you have to go check on the dying man; he may be gone!

All was still, autumn cold in the house. I stood still before the Red Room. As I placed my hand on the doorknob, I thought I could hear voices coming from the room in which Helena was sleeping. Softly I trod down the hall, placed my ear on her door and listened.

Marry me, then you'll be taken care of. The boy likes me too.

It was Morler's voice.

And if he gives you nothing?

The bright, brazen voice of the woman.

Without me he would never have gotten rich!

The woman replied that I was someone who was disillusioned with life. With someone like that, you never knew whether he was playing by the rules.

He who listens at the wall, hears his own shame first of all ...

She went on to say that my professor's disappearance had totally unhinged me and that such a person tended to avenge himself on the whole world.

There was a pause. Then noises, I couldn't believe it, the age-old noises, then, just a few minutes later, that voice again.

You're not an attractive man, Morler.

But I'll have money, and I love you.

Oh, Morler! And what if I clean you out and leave you high and dry?

Morler had no answer and kept silent.

And what if he gives you nothing?

He has to!

What are you doing here?

The boy had come out of his room and surprised me.

He was wearing his shabby Elvis-suit. It's the only one he has, I thought.

I'm listening, I said.

He who listens at the wall, hears his own shame first of all! the boy intoned.

I responded that I'd just heard that. Moreover, Helena's remarks had really hurt me.

Now we both listened, but there was nothing to hear, then a lot of chinking and clinking, as if someone were softly tapping on glass.

Look there, we heard Helena exclaim, the bullfinch is pecking at the window and wants to come in!

In the same instant Morler flung the door open. He was wearing a bathrobe. His face had reddened.

What's this, eavesdropping?

And what if I give you nothing, Morler? I cried out in an attempt to hide my shame. But behind him through the open door I saw Helena, standing naked at the window, looking at the bird who was pecking at the glass pane.

What, you're giving me nothing?

In another second Morler would've attacked me, so I took a step back.

Once I'm rich, I thought, I'll have nothing more to do with these people, and I'll also break the habit of occupying myself with myself.

The door to the Red Room opened and Edna stepped out.

He wants you all at his bed.

Now he's really dying, I thought.

Silently we walked down the hall in goose-step, me in the lead, then Morler, then the boy, then Helena, who'd thrown on a bathrobe. It was as if we were children going into the Christmas room.

Two men were with him as we entered. One was Greg, the notary, the other I didn't know.

Does he want to change his will again? I asked the notary and smiled.

Greg shook his head.

In the stillness we listened to the gasping, the rattling breath of the dying man. His face streamed with sweat, his mouth was open, his eyes closed, as if shut tight.

I hesitated to step closer, but the black cook shoved me in front of the bed, to the spot where I had so often stood during my visits.

Wilhelm must have sensed my proximity, for his eyes shot open.

The notary handed me a cloth. I immediately understood and used it to dab the dying man's brow and face. It was sweating everywhere, that poor desiccated body: *I am exhausted from my groaning, I dampen my divan with tears ...*

Wilhelm, I asked softly, as these words occur to me, has the time finally come?

And he nods and gives the signal for hot chocolate, and then the signal that he cannot speak, and the signals intermingle.

He's no longer breathing on his own, I think, rather death is making noises in his mouth; it's death doing this rattling and chinking.

He reached his hand out and smiled at me, embarrassed, as though ashamed to die; I didn't understand what it was he wanted, but the cook whispered to me: Take it, take his hand! And for the fraction of a second his hand clawed onto mine, I understood the meaning of life—and then forgot it again. There remained only the total bewilderment that death is actually happening.

Following an inspiration, I bent over him and kissed his brow—perhaps he'd been hoping for that the whole time he was still alive.

The second man, a doctor, approached the bed and closed his eyes. I loosened my hand from that of the dead man; it was warm; it went easily. Then I laid it on the bed alongside the body.

We were just standing around, aware that something had come to an end and that our lives would change. Then Edna began to cry, and the boy, who heretofore had merely observed everything with curiosity, saw this and broke into tears.

The undertaker would be there presently, said Greg.

Let's go into the kitchen and wait there, I declared with new authority.

Everything would roll off my back: my anxiety, my despondency, my who-gives-a-shit attitude—my whole character. I was rich.

19

I've calmed down. Even at the funeral I noticed it. Everything in the world is based on cause and effect – up to now I had denied this.

It was as if I had been transformed from a leptosome into an athletic type. As if I were now more philosophical, more stoic, and when Greg told me at the funeral—it took place in the park at the dead man's behest—about the suicide of the young doctor who had looked after Wilhelm for so long, I was shaken, unhappy even, over the fact that such a young man felt he had to leave this life; but I nevertheless felt an inner necessity to reconcile this fact with a certain scheme of cosmic order.

The burial took place right on the next day. Greg had managed to keep the press at bay. The notary took care of everything else, having black suits brought in for Morler and me, and for Helena a black mourning dress and a black hat with veil. Only the boy was forgotten and stood at the grave in his white Elvis-suit.

While Greg spoke a few words, we heard a car race through the park and up to the house at great speed and then slam on the brakes. Two men jumped out of the old car.

Greg had finished. One of the undertakers handed him a clarinet, and, at the dead man's request, he began to play "Petite Fleur"; as the melancholy melody wafted through the air, we were distracted by the two men moving toward us as fast as they could.

If they've come on account of Grissmann's inheritance, I said in a low voice as I approached them, they've come too late. The issue was decided a week ago. Still, I knew how it feels to lose, and they should stay for the funeral meal.

I'd spoken German and they nodded, one of them weeping, as the notary blew the final high notes.

We threw dirt onto the casket, I first of all, going by priority.

The light, I thought, as we sat in the kitchen at the funeral meal, the light. How completely different than in the mother house. There it's soft and sad, and how much more beautiful a lost home is than none at all.

Greg advanced me money and advised me to leave the country ASAP, to avoid being caught without a visa. He said Morler too should clear out, in the best case by tomorrow. We should take the same route back to Canada.

Ah, Greg, I said magnanimously, give Helena some money too, so she can get back to Europe. She was counting on getting an inheritance, and now she stands before us destitute.

As we're discussing this during the meal, Helena is sitting between us listening to everything. Her face expressionless, all she does is urge her son to fill his plate a second time with the good food, as though sensing hard times to come.

Good, says Greg, it's your money, Georg. He finds it awkward to discuss the matter openly.

You played "Petite Fleur" beautifully, I commend him, to help him get over his embarrassment. And, with a decisiveness that astonishes even me, be it America or my good fortune speaking through me, I add: If you have any cash on you, give it all to me and we'll leave immediately.

A half hour later we were on the road, riding refreshed across the vast landscape.

Morler drove. We were quiet. Mostly I looked out or paged through the little book, a booklet, actually a pamphlet, a thin notebook, that I had retrieved at the last moment from the dead man's commode drawer, furtively, together with the disk showing Helena.

"Vanishing Children's Culture in the German-speaking World."

Yes, I wrote that once.

At least Wilhelm had taken notice of it.

Five minutes before the world was made /

I shuffled across a potato glade ...

We rode into the twilight through endless fields. At one point I thought I recognized the spot where I had helped Helena out with gas. Then—it was already almost dark and Morler was driving more slowly—just off the highway I noticed a tree standing alone in which a gaggle of birds was nested. They reminded me of the bullfinch that had kept us company in the death house. How long ago that all now seemed! And, looking at the birds, I recalled what Edna once told me: that the bullfinch in particular was forced to steal sausages from the kitchen, since nature no longer provided sufficient nourishment for it …

Hey, Morler! I hooted. Here's the field you ran through, almost jeopardizing our mission!

It was now dark in the car, so I couldn't see his face, and he just kept driving, in silence, faster than before, and I thought I could hear him gnashing his teeth. Miles later he said something.

Outside the moon rose, the American moon, gigantic and red.

Will I get my money?

Yes, I answered.

Yet I noticed, even while speaking, that I wasn't sure.

In the Backofen Settlement

20

At the Berlin airport, I said goodbye to Morler, telling him he would hear from me, splitting the money I got from Greg with him, at most a few thousand dollars, and walking off leaving him standing there.

I still see him before me, that hulking baldheaded man in his trench coat, how he looks after me in vain, cash in hand.

These days when I think about that, I'm moved by this picture of helplessness, but back then I believed I owed it to my newfound wealth to no longer have any anxiety over such goodbys.

You're still practicing, I thought, as I disappeared into the crowd.

Then I took the bus to the Hilton, settled my bill (they accepted dollars) and picked up my luggage. I wasn't going back to the At Home Lodging House. Everything I left there was easily replaceable, and boasting of my fortune to Gregory didn't interest me. My car I left parked at the curb.

After all this time, you'll be seeing the mother house again.

I was still a young man, thirty-eight, a drifter, never far from total collapse.

Now I returned to my home city, changed by a strange destiny into something totally different. It almost seemed to me as if I were awakened after a long sleep and found myself turned into an old man, or as if I'd been wounded or crippled on the battlefield and were now allowed to go home.

A young woman sat next to me on the train, in second class. She smiled at me. But I wanted time to think and switched to first. Yep, the seats here were wider and softer, the head supports upholstered in white fabric.

The conductor came.

That's a second-class ticket you've got there.

I'll gladly pay the extra charge, I answered him straight in his stern face. I'll even pay double.

That was forbidden, he answered.

I pulled money out of my pants pocket, the thick wad of dollar bills and the euros I had exchanged, and counted out the required sum onto his hand.

All at once his grim face struck me as troubled; maybe he had suffered some terrible misfortune, something having nothing to do with my behavior.

I'll give serenity, I thought, after he moved on. You want serenity too, and can have it now that you're rich.

The German landscape whizzed by. My face became gray, the chameleon effect. Observation alone will never get you to the core of things. This thought, from my old research days, now occurred to me again: How well it suited my gray face.

As we sped through the tunnels of the Central Uplands, I was possessed by the longing for another time: the longing for the trip through America's fields, when nothing had yet been decided, and I was neither poor nor rich.

I got out in the early afternoon. I'm afraid of the afternoon, specifically the hours between two and four. They are hours during which I find I have to transform myself, into a werewolf, say, or a professor of dentistry, or an investigator of lost children's sayings—something.

So, I had wound up here. Bicycles were everywhere. The station square was full of them. This is where my parents lived, this is where my wife lived, in the mayor's house. This is where Krautmann lived before he disappeared. I felt the wad of cash in my pocket. I would've liked to sleep now, to forget myself and the universe for a while at least. But it was too early for sleep.

There were bus stops at the station square, with passengers waiting at the bays. Undecided as to what to do, I walked over to the bay where most of them were standing. The people waiting with me were shabbily dressed, and when I looked over to bay number ten, those waiting there were better dressed, and looked less dull.

The number nine bus pulled in and I persuaded myself it would lead me to adventures.

I said I wanted to go to the Backofen Settlement, but that the sign outside on the bus said something different. The nine bus used to go to Backofen. I added that I'd been away for a long time and asked whether that had changed.

It's not "Backofen" anymore, said the lady driver, smiling at my ignorance. These days we say "Wennfelder Garten."

Zip it up, someone behind me shouted.

I asked if the Grissmann House was still standing.

The driver said she wasn't familiar with it.

No, no, it's still there, asserted the man behind me, and pushed forward. It's in the old city.

The bus was crowded; I had to stand. The pushy guy had taken the last free seat.

We rode through the industrial section, passing an endless series of gas stations and fast-food joints. The bus stopped more often than I remembered; the narrow streets were full of potholes; it got more and more crowded around me; and I had to pick my light luggage up off the floor to keep it from getting stepped on. The money in my pants pocket pressed against the woman, and I looked her in the face to divine whether she might not steal it. But those were old-time anxieties: A rich person couldn't care less if you steal money from him.

It's so close, the woman said, as she was hurled against me by a bump in the street.

She was young, smaller than me, and looked up at me, her head poised back at that angle typical of women who mean to provoke a kiss. She smiled apologetically; she was missing a tooth.

Am I right, I asked, is this the nine bus to Backofen Settlement?

Then we came to the woods that conceal the settlement from the eyes of the city, and we were there.

I stood there at the bus stop to orient myself and watched the woman as she walked down the street. How easily I could've treated her to a new tooth with my money. With this new tooth, I thought, she'd be beautiful enough for me.

I hadn't been here for three years. The long, four-story tenement blocks with the pointed roofs and the attic rooms just beneath, the areas of lawn in front of the buildings, transformed by lack of care and romping children into large circles of reddish, hard-packed earth—that's how I remembered the place. However, I could now see that the houses must have been repainted in the intervening years, but that, through weather and the passage of time, almost everything had gone back to the way it was when I knew it long ago. A new bank branch had been added to the main square. Before that, Armbruster, a failed medievalist, had run a small grocery store there. I'm a philosopher and have my livelihood! That sonorous, somewhat rough voice of his, which he used to give this lie a veneer of truth. Yes, if I had only listened to his voice back then, and not also seen his bent figure, I would've believed him.

You could withdraw money from this branch for the rest of your life, I thought. But all I wanted to do was pay up my back rent. Then I would turn my back on this city.

At the far end of Backofenstraße, I reached the house where I was registered. Already from a distance I could see that it was the only one that had not been renovated: the kids playing ball near the front façade, the mothers laughingly watering the flowerbeds—it was only because I knew the mural that I was able to reconstruct it through these faded remnants. The blue plastic bag was still hanging in the big tree, blown up into it years ago during a storm. I was gripped by a certain joy over the world's immutability.

Had Armbruster not cheated his customers, had he not, following his first fall, experienced another fall, even deeper? A long time ago, while still a professor, I listened to one of his lectures: "The Image of the Goddess Fortuna in the Late Middle Ages."

No amount of money could ever erase all these memories.

There were some new names on the doorbell panel, mostly foreign. I still had my house key and unlocked the door.

I snuck past my landlord's apartment, just as I had so often done back then on account of my back rent. The musty odor coming from the apartment had increased over the years. Then I raced up the stairs, suddenly gripped by anxiety that the attic key might no longer work.

The tightness of Europe oppressed me, the air I had breathed in America was denied me. Here there would be no bullfinch singing outside the window.

Finally I stood before my door. The lock had not been changed; my old business card, "Georg Grissmann, Homeland Researcher," was still fastened to the door-frame with thumbtacks.

When I opened and immediately recognized everything, I was moved by the simple household, and an inexplicable envy of myself, at how I had been then, rose up in me. My bed, my table, my chair, my closet. The bit of linen I owned. In the kitchen alcove the teapot and cup. The dust of three years. Pushed through under the door several letters from my landlord. Electricity and water had not been turned off.

I put my bag down. In order not to give my feelings too much time, I went down the stairs and rang. The shuffling, the coughing, then the eye trained on the spy hole.

Who's there?

You can see for yourself, Herr Bausinger, I answered laughing.

He removed the chain lock and I could hear him open the first bolt.

Who?

Then came the second bolt, and he opened the door. He stood before me, smaller than my memory of him, somewhat stooped, in his cardigan and plaid slippers, the little hair he had carefully combed, his eyes opened wide behind his glasses.

Herr Grissmann!

Don't say a word, don't slaughter any fatted calves, I replied, I've come to settle up my back rent.

I noticed from my manner of speaking that it had to be past four, so I was no longer in thrall to the afternoon.

It's Herr Grissmann, he wants to pay his rent! Bausinger called into the apartment.

Naturally his wife would be sitting in the living room wanting to know every detail.

How much is it? I asked in the doorway, loud and clear, so that Bausinger's wife in the living room could hear it.

The bank transfers came for two years, then nothing for the last six months, the man answered.

So how much is it?

He'd written it down, answered Bausinger.

It's seven hundred and fifty, you could hear the old lady's voice croak. Surely she was sitting in the living room, ensconced on her high easy chair, her throne.

That's right, seven hundred and fifty, Bausinger repeated.

That much! I exclaimed with feigned concern.

Suddenly I thought I could hear the unlovely song of the bullfinch and no longer knew where I was.

Let him in!

Again the imperious, insolent squawking of the bird.

Come in, said Bausinger in a nasty tone, staring at the wad of money I had pulled from my pocket like a working stiff.

He walked in front of me, slowly, and I remembered the old waiter in Berlin who could play at being old so provocatively. At the moment, I wasn't sure if I wouldn't rather have been there.

Frau Bausinger sat in her living room, quite erect, a queen. But now, as I stepped closer, I saw that she was sitting in a new, even higher, armchair. As I counted out the money on the coffee table, bill by bill—at each new bill I put down, they nodded in agreement—it struck me that it wasn't the old coffee table. I looked around: The entire living room was newly furnished, and, in the spot where earlier the lamp had stood next to the sofa, there now stood a vertical rod with a birdcage.

Letting my eye scan the room, I had interrupted the counting-out of the money, and the woman signaled to her husband to keep me focussed on the remaining count.

Isn't it beautiful in here? the woman asked, as I finished paying my debt, everything's new, everything's renovated!

Yes, I answered, and I especially like the parrot.

It was the first thing they acquired after winning the lottery, the couple said together. Their aged voices trembled with pride.

Then you would now be rich, I asked?

They held their tongues in embarrassment, filled with anger over tipping their hand.

I asked whether the parrot had ever been in America, since he had squawked earlier exactly like a bird there.

They shook their heads, no doubt anxious to get rid of me after having given away their secret. Now, I thought, they probably believed I had them under my thumb.

I asked them whether there was still a store in the settlement, acting as though I had forgotten all about their lotto windfall. Armbruster had closed, I said, and I wanted to pick up a few things to eat, cheese, sausage, butter and bread, also some beer or wine to drink. Maybe light up a candle for dinner to celebrate my homecoming.

Tell him! From her throne on high the woman pointed down at the man.

Armbruster has opened a secret store, said Bausinger. After prison he came back and now has a secret store in the basement of House Two.

Good, so I'll be going over there now and disturb you no longer.

You won't give us away, will you? I could hear them call after me from the apartment.

No, I answered, adding on a whim: only if it should become necessary.

Bausinger walked me to the door. It was almost dark in the vestibule and I couldn't see the landlord's face clearly. Not until I opened the apartment door, and light streamed in from the stairwell, could I see his fear of me.

21

House Two—what was the story there? A child had lived there, the child of Krautmann's cleaning lady. Go and interview this child, the professor had said; he was withdrawn, but that could be because he felt out of place when his mother would take him with her to her cleaning job. So I went to the Backofen Settlement for the first time, bought some sweets at Armbruster's, also thought about flowers for my mother, and then hit pay dirt: The kid recited four brand-new sayings for me, as yet undocumented in the literature.

Now once again I stood before House Two. The door was ajar, someone having placed a small stone between the threshold and the door, making it impossible for the mechanism to close the door. House Two was like House One, so I instantly found the entrance to the cellar. The stairs were lit by pale neon light, which went out as soon as I hit the cellar hallway. One of the doors to the cubbyholes stood open. A soft yellow light coming from inside fell upon the otherwise dark corridor. A tape recorder was playing classical music, very low, hardly more than a whisper: As I moved closer, I recognized the "Summer" sequence from Vivaldi's Four Seasons.

I went in. Armbruster had cobbled together two of the cubbyholes and made a tiny store out of them for himself. The counter consisted of a door leaf, placed atop two boxes, behind which and all over the place goods were stacked.

Ah, a customer, Armbruster greeted me with a smile.

I told him I'd just returned from a trip and needed some basic supplies.

Without answering, he began to select items from the variety of his wares, laying the selection on the counter: a carton of fresh milk, brown sliced bread, butter, two kinds of cheese. Finally, he added a bachelor's pack of Italian salami to the mix.

Then Armbruster asked me whether I hadn't sat in on one of his lecture courses many years ago, always in the first row. As he did so, he held up two brands of tea before me, one of which I was to choose.

You also need eggs and honey for breakfast!

Yes, I heard him lecture back then, I said. Him, but mainly Krautmann.

He smiled. His face, which was red and somewhat ill-tempered in my memory, had become paler, but also more relaxed, his countenance that of a philosopher.

He noticed that I was studying his face without inhibition, and it was too late to act as though I were merely looking straight ahead and his head just happened to be there. Armbruster stood up straight and looked me in the eye. The slightly stooped vendor's posture had fallen away from him.

I've been in the slammer, you know that, don't you?

Yes, I know. Twice, actually.

He asked whether I remembered the expression. Nobody uses it anymore, he said, only here in the settlement you'll hear it now and then.

I still need wine and beer, I said, then I'll pay.

He put the drinks in front of me and mentioned the price, which seemed low to me.

I think that's too cheap, I went on. I pretended to feel around in my pocket, so as not to bring out the whole wad as I had just done at Bausinger's, and pulled out a bill, setting it down in front of him.

You've become rich, haven't you? said the grocer, without looking at me, as he handed me my change. You come back to your home a rich man. One notices it immediately.

I told him I'd be back tomorrow and that then he should hold me to the correct prices.

I set prices as I like, answered Armbruster.

Outside it was twilight time, a light that had always pleased me in the settlement, more melancholy than in any other place. The uniform houses seem to grow in this light, and to become lighter as they do, almost transparent. The paper bags full of groceries were heavy, and I took pleasure in the burden I had to schlep from House Two to House One. I intentionally walked more slowly, in order to prolong the precious moment of coming home, but also perhaps to stay in the street longer and possibly run into the girl with the missing tooth again.

I wanted to get home at the last instant, at the interface between dusk and darkness. If we could just do everything with the same willingness, do research the same as washing our hands, we would be happy. That was a thought from an earlier day, before I became rich, and as I climbed the steps to my attic room, I asked myself whether it was my own or one of Krautmann's.

I pursued this thought as I went about cleaning the apartment. The smell of the floor boards I'd wiped with a damp cloth induced a euphoria in me; dusting the few sticks of furniture took only a moment. I made the bed, astonished at the whiteness of the bed linens; in the kitchen alcove, I unpacked my groceries, plugged in the little fridge and started it up. In the past whenever I would think of this apartment, it always seemed to me as though it must be desolate, a place one hates and leaves forever. Now it was different. I had opened the dormer window. Wind came in, damp and with the smell of the woods that separate the city from the settlement.

There was only one of almost everything here. One plate, one spoon, one fork, one knife. Cups were the only thing I had two of. From my hideaway I retrieved my most precious possession: a laced tablecloth from the eighteenth century that I had stolen from the Grissmann House linen closet.

Now that you have so much, you'll bring it back, I thought.

I lit a candle and set about dinner.

How the candle light once again refined the bobbin lace! How delicious Armbruster's simple fare tasted! How I was home and yet free!

Later, lying in the freshly made bed, I could hear through the open window the soft, almost watery cry of the European owl coming from the woods. The cool night air wafted in, causing me to shiver with pleasure under the warm spread. I would be asleep in no time. Till then my plan was to think about Scott and Amundsen and their race to the South Pole.

Berlin he found too big / so off to France he danced a jig /

France wasn't to his taste, so home he went again in haste …

22

The next morning I walked through the settlement as though it belonged to me. It was a beautiful autumn day, one of those days on which being alone is a great gift. A thick fog hung over the separating woods, and I thought: You can go in there too, right into the fog, but just as well along the sun-drenched streets between the houses. A hearty good mood came over me; I squinted at the still low-hanging sun, greeted complete strangers, cherished a kind of love for them.

Careful, I mouthed to myself, otherwise there'll be tears in the offing. Still the euphoria persisted. I thought of Amundsen. The south pole, he reached it! Scott I had totally forgotten.

I passed House Eleven, then a little kiosk that I didn't recall from earlier. An older couple was standing in front of it, the woman with a styrofoam cup of coffee, the man with a bottle of beer. The morning sun was shining on the short, squat bottle, and the reflected light blinded me.

I greeted them; they nodded back shyly. Then—I had already moved on—I suddenly realized who it was standing inside the kiosk. The forest fog could wait …

I said I was undecided whether I should get coffee or beer.

With her left hand she extended the cup to me, with her right the bottle, then again the cup, and again the bottle. I pointed to the cup; she filled it and handed it to me.

I told her I'd be back that evening; then I would choose the beer.

I blew into the coffee and drank.

I mentioned that I wanted to go right into the woods, into the fog.

She wiped the counter and didn't answer.

I told her her coffee was bad but passable.

She said she was new and not yet familiar with the machine.

I told her I had just returned here yesterday.

This is not the way, I thought; you could go on talking like this forever.

I said I would come there every morning for coffee.

We saw the fog as it slowly came upon us from the woods.

What will you give me if I spring for a new tooth for you?

She stared mutely over at her two customers standing at the bar table, then raised her head a little.

A new tooth would cost one-thousand-five-hundred euros.

So much? I heard myself ask. Again I had forgotten that I was rich.

How old are you? How old are you, Britta?

I had read her name from the name tag she wore on her jacket.

Nineteen. And you?

Thirty-eight. My wife ran off and left me for the mayor. She's now the mayor's wife. I asked her whether she wouldn't rather be twenty-five, looking so sad as she did?

I didn't know what I wanted and just jabbered on. Just wait for the next answer, I thought. If you don't like it, move on.

She said she wasn't sad, just disappointed. Yesterday she asked her boss to put her in one of his kiosks in the city center, at the marketplace or the university, but he rejected her request. The way she looked, she could only be considered for the Backofen Settlement.

It became a bit darker; the first patches of fog moved in front of the sun. Even that looks beautiful, I thought.

I wondered what good would come of her new tooth. What can one expect in return for a new tooth?

(But) I shouldn't make fun of her!

She had spoken loudly, and the couple at the bar table were looking over at us, full of expectation over what was to come, right down to the inconceivable occurrence.

She was trying to save, said Britta, but you couldn't earn anything here; yes, she was a participant in profit-sharing but had no more than three hundred euros saved up.

I answered that I found it wonderful to be chatting with her here while the fog gilded itself as it moved in front of the sun, allowing our gaze to sweep over the downtrodden grassy patches between the houses. How long had she been saving for it? I asked following a pause.

One year.

I felt like talking about myself, as I'd done so often in America.

My wife's been living in the mayor's house for three years, I said.

How stupid to talk about your wife when you're trying to flirt with someone new!

Do you know the Grissmann House? I asked. The big old house in the old city?

Everyone knows it, she answered, even here in the settlement.

No, I thought, don't say another word about it.

In a moment the fog will be swallowing up your customers, I said, pointing at the shroud of mist that had now reached the older married couple.

You've made me sad; I think you should go now! she cried out angrily and made a fist. And in case I had any money left, she added, I should be careful. They say there are rich people living in the settlement, incognito, people you had to watch out for.

I said I'd be heading off into the woods now, into the fog. But if she liked, she could visit me; I lived in House One in the attic.

I had already taken a few steps towards the fog when I turned around again:

Could she remember any children's sayings? I would collect any sayings.

She looked out into the fog and pondered.

Eyes of brown are dangerous,
but in love are good for us,
eyes of green are serpentine
and of love none can be seen.
Eyes of blue are sunstar true,
Love to kiss and flirt with you.

She hadn't thought of that for years, the girl hollered, then laughed and clapped her hands. I walked back and looked her in the face: Her eyes were blue.

I didn't know that one, I lied; I'd be sure to write it down for my collection. And maybe she could think of other ditties to gladden my researcher's heart.

You'll be going to the south of France, to the Cote d'Azur, to a villa on the sea, I thought, but before that let's enjoy the woods, the fog, the settlement, Armbruster, Bausinger and this girl too, one more time.

Oh, by the way, I asked her as I was leaving, have they torn down the bratwurst stand in the separating woods?

She nodded.

I headed for the woods. Soon the kiosk and houses disappeared in the fog behind me. Visibility in the forest amounted to no more than a few paces, but years ago I had knocked around here often, with friends, though mostly by myself, and stuck to the path.

Of course, straight ahead was the upward slope at the end of which the woods opened up. On clear days one emerged from the darkness and saw the city lying beneath one: church and river, town hall and the roof of the Grissmann House. Today, however, on the thirteenth of October, the day after my return, everything was lost in a sea of fog. I wanted to picture to myself all that I couldn't see now, but I wasn't able to. Instead of that, I all at once became aware of how I myself looked. Almost painfully my own image loomed before my eyes; it was as though I were using the fog to mirror myself: a tall and strapping blond man whose youthful features were beginning to be sharpened by age …

Just that morning while shaving I had taken a look in the mirror. Wealth has yet to chisel itself into your features; one doesn't see it in you yet, I'd thought.

I had yet to see the city and turned around.

Armbruster, I said, as my eyes adjusted themselves to the faint light and I saw his slightly stooped ascetic figure rise from the camping chair, I need something to eat. What do you recommend?

I was cold from the fog, from the woods. I should long ago have changed my thin, shabby clothing.

The grocer answered that he had cans of ravioli, assuming my intention was to play the pauper. For the more well to do among the settlement residents there were quite different delicacies available.

Those I don't need, I cut him short. He was to give me a can of ravioli.

He put it down before me with a smile.

Did I know, he asked, that, while in prison, he had written a study on ethics. If I liked, he could lend it to me. But if Britta pays you a visit, he said changing the subject, wouldn't it be a good idea to have champagne in the house?

Fine, give me a bottle, I heard myself say.

I'll give you a cold one; evening is coming on. By the way, Brigitte, Britta's mother, is the more beautiful woman by far. In those endless nights in prison it was only thinking of her and the work on my ethics that enabled me to endure being locked up.

I didn't want to hear anything about that and told him so.

Oh, Grissmann! You're just not friendly to people! Yes, I know who you are and I know your story.

I would like to stay here in the settlement, I said, but that would be difficult if the owner of the only shop had a negative attitude towards me. Don't you like me, Armbruster, do you maybe even hate me?

No, he said. And he'd sell me the champagne for less than the other rich people here.

Good, I said, taking my purchases. And occasionally I would be needing someone to talk to; maybe I'd come back here and even take a look at his ethics study.

Yesterday I hadn't completely unpacked, and as I went about it after dinner, I spotted the booklet and the disk I'd brought back with me from America.

I paged through my work. Yes, indeed, I had accomplished a little in life and as I again read the sayings I had salvaged, I was proud of myself. But the afternoon came and made me weak: All of my work at that time suddenly struck me as superfluous, all my pride was gone, and I decided instead to play the disk.

A shoe store in a strip mall. A young salesgirl is alone in the store unpacking shoes and decorating the display window. Outside a Porsche pulls up and stops in the no-parking space. She pays no attention to the young man who gets out of the car. He's carrying a bouquet of flowers. The fellow comes in and wants to give her the flowers, but she doesn't accept them. He invites her to come with him on a trip to nowhere in particular. She says no. Even if she didn't have to work now, she wouldn't want to go anywhere with him. If he didn't want to buy shoes, he had better get going. He gives up and leaves the store. Outside, in front of the shop window, he wants to signal hi to the girl again. Just then a lady biker rushes by and knocks him on his keister. The man lies there on the ground bleeding from a wound on his head. The salesgirl runs out. She guides the dazed fellow into the store. She fetches a gauze bandage from the first-aid cabinet and binds his wound. Then she kisses him. She undresses him, then herself. She rides him.

By that time the afternoon threat was over. Still, I was feeling lonely. My mission to use my wealth to give my life stability, a new direction, loomed over me like a tidal wave. Tomorrow I would watch the film a second time; maybe I had overlooked something; maybe it had a secret message.

Shortly before six it occurred to me that I only owned one glass for sipping champagne. All at once I felt as if there were a noise in my head, a faint scraping and sliding, as though by mice, as though by animals. Then I remembered that I had earlier stuffed a wad of cotton into the bell button so as to make the bell inaudible in the attic. The noise is outside, I thought; someone's pressing the doorbell—but the bell can only ring raspingly.

When I opened, Bausinger stood in front of me.

I was expecting someone else, I said, a young girl. Very pretty, even if she was missing a front tooth.

They'd thought it over, said Bausinger, as he furtively scanned the attic: they could accommodate me on the back rent. If I kept knowledge of their lottery winnings to myself, they would accommodate me. How well, how carefully they had kept their windfall secret, that is, until I came along. They would remit half the rent to me!

Money is not important to me, I answered.

What if you could live here for free?

I could see his desperation and shrugged my shoulders, finally agreeing with him.

Bausinger said he realized it was no longer customary, but he thought we should shake hands on it anyway. Will you hold firm to our arrangement?

Yeah, yeah, I answered airily and removed my hand from his.

Then he said he was off to tell his wife the good news.

I responded by telling him that, first, I wanted to ask him another personal question. Namely, how did he feel now about his rage and hatred of the poor? Did it all just roll off him right after his lottery win? Or was he still feeling that old rage against the rich, even though he was now one of them?

Bausinger said that in his wife's case it was over with immediately, while with him it had taken longer, even that it was still ongoing. Whenever he would hear about the secretly rich at the kiosk or at Armbruster's, the old rage would still surge up in him.

We heard footsteps on the stairs. As Bausinger opened the door and stepped out, the girl squeezed past him. There's no way he didn't feel her breasts. She was wearing tight black lederhosen, a black T-shirt and over that a short leather jacket embellished with silver studs.

After viewing the film, I was no longer looking for adventure and wasn't sure if I wouldn't have preferred to get rid of Britta.

So this is how you live!

I asked if she was disappointed.

She didn't have it any better, she answered. House Thirteen. It was noisier there, coming from the street, and dirtier than here in One.

I offered her the chair and sat down on the stool myself, but then stood up again and lit the candle. It was getting dark outside. We were silent.

At first she didn't want to come, she said, staring into the candle flame. But Armbruster told her I had bought champagne; this made her curious.

I saw the gap between her teeth.

No, I hadn't bought any champagne, I heard myself say. I told her my first name and suggested that we use "du."

She said her boyfriend Jacko knocked her tooth out. They weren't going together anymore.

Jealousy?

She didn't answer. She'd become sad. And even if sadness in youth is not so heavy as it is later, she infected me with it. Anything sexual, the whole idea of foreplay, was suddenly repugnant to me.

Armbruster had warned her, she said after a while. He'll promise you a new tooth, then you'll have to go to bed with him.

Where did Armbruster get that idea?

It's because I'm a bad person, she said. Armbruster could tell.

Yeah, I answered, it may well be that I'm a bad person. By the way, I lied to you, I actually did pick up champagne.

I gave her the only glass and used the cup myself. We touched glasses, both in a melancholy mood. I began to talk about my parents, about the Grissmann House, my ex-wife, my professor's disappearance …

That's all so remote, she replied.

How much can you scrape up?

Three hundred.

Here's five hundred, I said, and laid the money on the table. Then I told her to go.

Couldn't she finish her drink, she asked. It was so delicious.

No, go now. Come back tomorrow.

She took the money and I pressed her towards the door. Without a word of good-bye, we split.

Moments later someone started up a loud ruckus in front of House One. I opened the window to hear better.

Grissmann, you swine!

It was a woman's voice.

I closed the window and went to bed early.

Towards morning I woke up from restless dreams. I felt all over myself to see if maybe I'd been transformed. But my back was no harder than before, my stomach no softer, my extremities obeyed me; they were still those of a human being.

No, a glorious chain of days lay before me. I would shape them freely, like a child at play.

23

I cannot escape the city. The little bank branch in the settlement is not suited to my needs—it would arouse too much notice in Backofen. Besides that, I need new clothes. By the way, I've told Armbruster about my past. What are you gonna do, he exclaimed, travel the country with your lecture, show up in village restaurants and community halls and let yourself be splattered with tomatoes? How low can you go?

Yeah, I've been marked by life. Man is the plaything of the gods.

This made him reflective. He said he'd sell me the next bottle of champagne for settlement price. Man as plaything of the gods … How long it had been since he'd heard this beautiful proposition!

He'd become maudlin and I was afraid he'd start to cry.

Here, take it, he said, take it as a gift.

He grabbed a bottle from his stash and handed it to me.

And be nice to Britta.

That evening I opened the bottle given me by Armbruster and thought about what it must be like to be him. Britta was totally off my mind so I was surprised when I heard the doorbell ring and there she stood before me.

She said she didn't want to come, and didn't want to come in now, but that she had to warn me. Her ex-boyfriend had been telling everybody that he wanted to beat me to a pulp. Only if she were to come back to him would he temper justice with mercy. But she didn't want to go back to him and so I should keep an eye out, or, in the best case, leave.

Again she was out of breath from climbing the stairs, and with her blue eyes and her short, pertly cut blonde hair struck me as even more beautiful than before.

Hang on, I said, holding her by the arm, since she was already set on running down the stairs, were you the one who, one night recently, cursed me in the street? "Grissmann, you swine, Grissmann, you swine!" I shouted, aping her female voice.

And if I was, she answered insolently, trying to free herself, and if I was? I stood forewarned, she said, and now she had to go!

To Jacko, no doubt? I pumped her.

She shook her head, but I pulled her into the attic by the arm.

No need to cry out, I wasn't going to hurt her, I said. Here, have some champagne!

She lowered her head, walked to the door, then turned around, took the glass from my hand without a word and drank.

Here, I said, here's another two hundred for you.

Suddenly I felt the urge to harm her and pushed her out the door.

I went to the window, opened it and waited to hear if the girl would curse me again. The cold night air was intoxicating. However, there was nothing to hear but Britta's hurried footsteps and so I shouted out the window myself: Grissmann, you swine! Grissmann, you sow!

It was as if along with wealth I had also acquired great physical powers, and I consequently dismissed the girl's warning as irrelevant. But just to be on the safe side, I decided I would consult with Armbruster tomorrow. No way did I want to leave Backofen so soon! Didn't I have everything I needed here? A philosopher as a conversation partner, free lodging, a young woman to whom I could play the lovestruck older man, the woods, the fog, the Fall.

It was ten o'clock and the bottle was still half-full. I wanted to have a look at my booklet before going to sleep. Or study the behavior of the shoe salesgirl a second time. I couldn't decide and went to bed.

I will not escape the city. You'll approach it in small steps, so I thought in the morning, as I looked out at the woods in which fog and sun carried on their daily combat. First to the bank, after that a short walk through the old city, avoiding the house in question, perhaps passing by the institute as well. (Business lawyers had occupied the place since my time.)

He who is rich will not die. I had dreamt this sentence. I was sitting on a bridge over a river, my legs crossed, a greasy cap on the pavement next to me. Pedestrians were coming and going, and one man stopped, wanting to toss a gold coin into the cap, but it missed its mark and began to roll. I went to grab it but it was already in the river. The almsgiver, however, said to his companion: He who is rich will not die.

I finished my coffee and decided to go into the woods.

Again I stood on the spot where, recently, due to the fog, I was unable to see the city. Today the view was good, the air clear and cool, of a kind that makes faraway things appear closer.

On the way here, I'd thought about my fortune, how large it might be and how much one might need to point one's life in a new direction, and how much one might need in order to go back to one's life path, to the point where one thought to have chosen the wrong direction; in order finally to arrive at the desired goal, the one missed at the time.

Again and again, jaybirds with their carping tore me away from my thoughts, or a fox who showed himself for a moment, or strangely shaped sun spots that had fallen through the half-defoliated trees onto the path strewn with multicolored leaves. Now the city lay before me within my grasp.

24

Two different things happened yesterday: I was mugged/ attacked and I was in the city.

In the morning I walked through the settlement. A few residents were out and about, you could easily observe them. Being in a pensive mood, I walked slowly and noticed from their glances that they were well along the way to forming an impression of me. But that image was still unfinished in their heads, and I was free. You must tell Armbruster about that, I thought, this observation would have to please someone like him.

I wanted to have lunch at the kiosk. First I got in line, but the line slogged along only very slowly. Then I saw that it wasn't Britta but a fortyish woman standing behind the counter, someone bearing a remote resemblance to the girl.

And what can I get for you?

She smiled, not a tooth missing. Now I could see that she had once been beautiful, but long since not the way she appeared in Armbruster's prison dreams.

Nothing, I answered and stepped aside for the person behind me.

The fellow behind me was wearing a lumberjack shirt, coarse boots and rugged blue pants. His voice was deep and booming. But his black hair was a little too dark not to be tinted, and his gait was that of an old man.

Yep, you're a lucky man, I exclaimed, as he moved a place ahead through my stepping out of line!

With these words I left the place.

Back home I read for a while. There was a lot in the slender book that struck me as totally new, much of it also sounding bogus, as if the author had not collected the sayings of the children but thought them up himself.

Later when I went to Armbrust's cellar, he already knew all about it.

What are you doing, Grissmann! he yelled at me before I could even greet him. His haggard face was trembling. Everybody was talking about it: how somebody had got on line at the kiosk, but then simply walked away. That was you?

So what if it was? I answered, what was so bad about it?

Come on, Grissmann! He shook his head in pity. So should he go around telling everybody that I let myself be splattered with tomatoes for money in the backrooms of inns in far-flung hamlets? Then people would be moved to accept me?

Whatever floats your boat, I answered. And another thing, Armbruster. If you were open every day, the days of the week would in future mean nothing to me.

He was always open, answered Armbruster.

There was no one in the store besides us, and

immediately Armbruster began to talk about his ethics, beginning with Aristotle, then moving on to eudaemonia, and how he—the first to do it, so far as he knew—had established a connection between ethics and humor…

His somewhat brittle voice resounded in the basement room; in a university auditorium it would've had a powerful effect on me. Here, however, I had a realization that made me sad.

Armbruster, I thought, I had taken you for a free spirit, a philosopher. Now I see that you're using your ethics, your work, to legitimize your existence. How tacky!

It was only out of pity that I listened to him further, though I noticed only too clearly that he was dreaming of rehabilitating himself on the basis of his own ethics.

That's wrong, I thought.

Soon after I left him, I was mugged. Attacked?

It was on the playground I crossed in order to get home with my groceries faster. The monkey bars, seesaw and swings were in poor shape, rusted and broken down. Pointy things, rusty iron parts jutted out all exposed. Not a single child was playing on this playground.

I noticed someone following me, and as I went to turn around, I heard a swishing sound and instinctively turned my head away, so that it was only on my shoulder that the stick landed with any pain. I'd dropped my grocery bag, and even as I turned around, I thought: Hopefully the bottles won't break, but at the same time I recalled that I was rich and strong. I punched the arm holding the stick—the stick fell to the ground. Then I turned the mugger's arm around and up his back. He howled with pain in the armlock.

It was a skinny twelve- or thirteen-year-old boy, in cheap sport gear.

What do you want from me?

He was a ruddy kid with very fair hair, and the white eyelashes several breeds of cow have.

He didn't answer.

What's your name? I yelled.

(He was the sort of kid you run into in passing in elementary school. They're gone in no time.)

He held his tongue, and I plied him—as in fairy tales—with a third question while shoving his arm a little higher up his back.

What did I do to you?

I had him well enough in hand that I could take a look around: not another person to be seen anywhere. The stick lying on the ground still had its bark. But one of its ends had initials carved into it, the bright wood showing: J.S.

Cat got your tongue, Jacko?

My shoulder hurt.

I could've kept the kid there that way for hours with one hand. I looked over at the forest to see if it was foggy.

Are you dumb?

I said that without thinking, but as his silence continued, I took this possibility more seriously. His nails were chewed up, his hands dirty, his fingertips yellow as with chainsmokers. Kids like him start smoking early, I thought.

I let him go, and he reached much too slowly for the stick that still lay on the ground near us. As I picked it up, he cut and ran, pausing once, however, to look longingly back at his stick.

Heretofore Backofen had always struck me as a paradise from which I would be driven by my fortune; still I wanted to defend it as long as possible.

I made a threatening move, and, tauntingly slowly, indeed, with casual impudence, he disappeared into House Five.

I liked the stick, it felt good in my hand, plus it was thicker and a little bent on its one side just above the initials, so that you could use it as a walking stick. I swung it back and forth—it could also be used as a weapon.

You've gained a victory, I thought; that's a part of paradise too. Only now did I become aware of how feverishly the adrenalin in my blood was seething; and, using the stick that was meant to whack me on the head as a walking stick, I hoofed it to the kiosk.

Britta wasn't there, nor was her mother. I decided to go into the city.

25

Again and again this scene has annoyed the hell out of me: A bus has just taken off, somebody comes running, too late; the doors of the bus are shut, the bus is rolling; disappointment etches itself on the face of the one locked out. Suddenly the driver stops, the door swings open, the latecomer is saved. And a mood takes hold in the bus as though something great has been accomplished, the driver a hero, and a wave of sympathy, almost of love, envelops the one who made it on.

Everybody's happy for a fraction of a second—but me. I don't care for this exuberance. And so I don't run when a bus is about to pull away from me, rather I bear the thought that not all are saved, however fast they may run.

Now the tandem bus is moving into the turning bay of Wennfelder Garten. Passengers are getting out. But I'm still fifty meters away. The first ones off are coming towards me. The doors are already closing. Another ten or fifteen meters still. The bus takes off, then stops again.

He's stopping, I think, the doors are opening. And I run. But just as I get there, the driver fools me, closing the doors again and driving on.

And I laugh, just as the driver no doubt laughs at me. For when you can exact vengeance anytime you like, like me, you tend to take things with a grain of salt.

Leaning on my stick, I watched the bus pull away. But the bus stopped yet again, the driver honked, and again I ran, cursing myself for doing so.

I get the biggest kick out of doing that with you people from Backofen, the driver said as he let me board.

And what if I make a mental note of you, I answered, and take my revenge?

Oh, that won't be so terrible.

The whole bus is bursting with laughter; even the man I let go ahead of me at the kiosk is there. And this guy, who merely plays at being strong, offers me his seat as a joke.

It's a half-hour ride to the Schimpfeck. That's where the bank I'm looking for is. And, just before I enter the bank, I pass by the Deutsches Haus. Once, many generations ago, it belonged to the Grissmann family; now it belongs to other people; it contains a hotel and a traditional pub.

How often my father took my mother and me there on holidays, and, although I could appreciate good food even at that age, I dreaded these outings. It seems that every time my father would enter the place in high spirits, but in the course of the meal would end up staring at the coats of arms on the wood-paneled wall, impervious to my mother's efforts to cheer him up, leaving his schnitzel unfinished. I was allowed to finish it, furious at my father for spoiling my schnitzel dinner with his moods.

Everything here was steeped in memory. My shoulder hurt as I pushed open the heavy glass door of the bank building.

I went to the reception desk, showed my ID card and demanded to speak to the director. The young man's glance scanned my shabby clothes; the sight of the stick irritated him.

With this stick I was beaten today, I said, adding that I was able to defend myself. Now it belonged to me.

Did I have an appointment?

I shook my head, violently, like a wild man who lives in the forest.

He said he would see if Dr. Gesellius had time for me.

Gesellius? I shouted. Thomas Gesellius?

My voice resounded throughout the lobby, and, by reason of the peculiarities of the architecture, it sounded as if I were trying to conjure up Gesellius like the Earth Spirit. I was shocked by the sound.

I was told that if I really were Grissmann, Dr. Gesellius wished to see me immediately.

I was led through the anteroom, past a secretary, into the director's office.

Gesellius, you old duffer, what are you doing here?

Yes, Georg, I'm a bank director now! What's that stick you have there?

I had it from Backofen, I said.

He gestured at two leather armchairs near his desk, and we sat down.

The most important thing was discretion, I said. Then I asked him if he had received the letter from the USA.

Yes. But, Georg, the amount of money is unimaginable!

I told him that only he, he alone in this city, was to know about it. Could he guarantee me that?

He would have to let one or two colleagues in on it, Gesellius answered.

He looks like he did in the old days, still a dandy: precisely the roll I had wanted to play when I stumbled onto Krautmann's team, and which I found occupied by him.

Are you happy here?

He was trapped, but happy, the bank director answered. In case I'd been away for a while and therefore didn't know: There was nothing new in the Krautmann case, he was still missing.

Coffee was brought in.

How did we stand with each other, Grissmann? he asked. Were we enemies? Competitors maybe, but certainly not enemies. He then admitted he had a little fear of me, now that I was powerful.

With your fortune you're hardly even human anymore, he added softly.

As a bank director you too must have money like matchsticks, no? I countered.

Chicken shit compared to yours! Gesellius exclaimed.

Then it occurred to me that he had headed up one of the more important projects at the institute; the word was that it would be quite a roll of the dice. Even Krautmann had let fall a remark about it, with something close to awe in his voice when he said it; the rest of us trembled with envy. It had to do with the dependence of regional patriotism on pecuniary circumstances. Certainly a heavyweight compared to my verses!

Will you be going to America? That's what he would advise, added the bank director, he would advise it in good faith!

I was dumbfounded by his advice and told him all about how much I was enjoying Backofen now and how I had no wish to leave.

But Gesellius wouldn't hear of it and interrupted me. He'd become angry—didn't he just now even threaten me with his fist?

If he had the authority, he'd ban me from the city, cried the bank director. Just go to America! Sow your wild oats there, not here!

He'd jumped up and stood over me threateningly; in no time he'd be on me like a rabid dog.

The stick, I thought. But Gesellius merely paced up and down, still breathing heavily, threatened me again with his fist and finally sat down.

You want to butt in. Don't do it! By character you're not strong enough for the power chance has given you.

This is a madman, I thought. Then it occurred to me that I had entertained quite similar thoughts.

What have I done, Gesellius, that you should hate me so?

I laughed. Even though his words had hurt me, still I was rich. I'm rich and I have the stick, I thought, and I grabbed it and played with it.

I don't hate you, he said, softening his tone. But I had to realize that I was just interfering here, just getting things all bolloxed up. The mayor was a friend of his, he said, a man who had brought about progress for the city, and the support of his wife was essential for the success of his plans. And *that* he saw jeopardized by my return. Ah, Georg, he said, changing the subject, what a wonderful time that was at the institute!

Doubtless in order to wipe the slate clean of his hateful outburst, he began to scan one of the children's verses I had collected at that time:

Banana, limetta—on the corner stands a man
Banana, limetta—he lures the girls as best he can

Come on, join in!

And I actually found myself doing it, flattered that he was quoting me—sort of—so that I chimed in:

Banana, limetta—he takes them home with him
Banana, limetta—he strips them on a whim—
Banana, limetta—he takes them off to bed—

We laughed so hard we couldn't speak.

Shit, man, Gesellius exclaimed, how much better he'd feel if I would promise him to keep out of sight here in the city from now on.

The secretary brought cognac in two brandy glasses.

Gesellius, did you just want to pound on me?

He shrugged his shoulders. Again he had that self-confident expression on his face, the one for which I used to envy him so.

He answered by asking if he might put a question to me. Why weren't you present at your father's funeral?

He's dead? I said that I hadn't heard anything about it, that I'd been in America.

He said they'd buried him in the city cemetery. The mayor had arranged it, there being so many Grissmanns interred there.

When was that, Gesellius?

He stood up as if he'd just thought of something, walked over to the desk and came back with a brown envelope in the one hand and a red book in the other.

Here was the cash money he was supposed to give me, as stipulated in the letter of the American branch office.

He handed me the envelope.

And here, this he wanted to give me personally. It was the project he had headed up back then. He had finally finished it and had it privately printed. By the way, he said, he needed to look at my ID card and get my signature.

I showed him the card, he took down the number, I signed.

I wished to leave now, I said, I wanted to be alone to reflect on my father's death.

Gesellius accompanied me to the exit.

He mentioned that the mayor had given a very beautiful eulogy in honor of my father.

What would be the loss, I wondered as I came out on the street, if I were never to see Gesellius again? If he had never existed at all?

Involuntarily I turned around one more time and looked up at his office window; it was as if I wanted to imprint on my mind the place where I had learned of my father's death. But just as I looked up, someone up there had stepped to the window and was threatening me with his fist.

26

I wandered through the city, repeating to myself over and over the sentence: You were at the wrong deathbed. This sentence kept grief at bay; but at some point the sentence's power would be used up and I would be delivered up helplessly to my feelings.

Aha, I thought in the historic pedestrian zone, people are stopping and turning towards me; you're probably talking to yourself out loud. I forced myself to keep the sentence on the level of thought.

I didn't want to go see my mother just now, so I took the route leading to the cemetery.

My mouth was dry and I had to clear my throat again and again, like someone who's spoken for too long using the wrong technique. Now I was passing the hospitals, already a long ways away from the Grissmann House: My breath was smoother, my gait became freer. I approached the cemetery almost nonchalantly.

The sentence was gone. In its place I began to create a picture of my father and his life, now that the two would be joined together forever. "De Grizzmans seyn scheene Leut," it reads somewhere in an old chronicle. My father quoted this often, sometimes seriously, sometimes laughingly. He himself was a pyknic type, a man of powerful, thickset physique. This type appeared in the Grissmann family much less often than the leptosome or the mesomorph, he said. And he was glad his son was a leptosome: That was right and proper for a Grissmann.

I arrived at the city cemetery and shook the gate. Too late – the cemetery was closed.

Even in my youth my father had struck me as ridiculous. I'd never experienced him as having a full head of hair, he was always a chrome dome. Now, as I once again shook the locked cemetery gate—as I did so, it gave forth a clear squeaking noise, two notes, high and melodic, like the whistling of an oriole—I regretted not having loved my father more, especially as a child; also that I, despite my riches, did not have it in me to ever make it up. I noticed I was weeping.

I still had the stick with me. It didn't suit my sorrow so I flung it against the cemetery wall. But it rebounded from the wall elastically, as if it wanted to come back to me.

Later, in a few days, I thought, you'll go into the city again and look up your mother along with the grave; buy some new clothes too. Now I wanted to return to the settlement. I'd walked maybe fifty meters when I turned around again.

It was already getting dark. No one was on the street, the cemetery wall shone freshly whitewashed. A great peace emanated from it. But the stick was lying in front of it on the sidewalk. Someone might trip over it, so I walked over to it and picked it up.

On the way to the bus station my throat was constricted. Every now and then I felt my cheeks to see if I'd been crying. I'd've certainly liked to cry again if it would've helped the feeling in my throat. Then I remembered a principle from my confirmation class, one that gave me anxiety at the time, through its brevity, its rawness: The wages of sin is death.

My father had attained the age of no more than seventy.

Behind the university, at the taxi stand, I once again realized that I was rich.

To the Backofen Settlement, I said to the drivers, who stood together next to their cabs smoking. With each drag their cigarettes glowed more brightly in the darkness, now from this one, now from that. In spite of my grief, I could tell that they'd been talking about fucking.

The wages of sin is death. Yes, this principle still gave me the creeps.

Take me to the bus station, to where the busses leave for the settlement.

Do you plan to continue on from there by bus? asked the cab driver, sounding pissed off.

No, I answered. But if by chance a certain girl was standing there, I intended to pick her up.

The driver coasted past the column of people waiting; Britta was not among them.

Aren't you afraid? I asked, as we drove through the separating woods, the headlights illuminating the ramrod-straight road. Aren't you afraid I might attack you? I told him I had taken the stick away from a boy who had come at me with it.

The trees bordering the street flew by in the headlights. At one point a deer appeared briefly.

No doubt you've sensed my anxiety, the driver replied. He said he'd been attacked one night on this stretch.

Just imagine, I suddenly said: About two weeks ago I was visited by a private detective. Since that night I've not had a single moment of boredom. Also, a week ago my father died, and it's only today that I learned of it.

We left the woods; the familiar silhouette of the settlement lay before us.

He asked if I wanted to be left off at a particular building, or rather at a bus stop so that no one would know right off where I lived.

At the bus stop, I said.

He stopped and we both got out, he included, to stretch a bit and rotate his head. I looked at him more closely in the streetlight. He was tall with long, thin limbs like a greyhound; his face had something foxlike about it. I might not ever see him again; maybe that's the reason I gave him a big tip.

There was no one on the street as I walked to my attic, using my stick as a walking staff. Thoughts about my father oppressed me, and, although at first I wanted to sit on the chair at my table, without turning the light on, I put it on anyway, to prevent the thoughts and memories from getting the upper hand. Like fish in a pond too small, they crisscrossed each other; indeed, the very thoughts about my father distracted me from my grief over losing him.

Again and again I looked at my watch without knowing why. But I had received this watch from my father at confirmation, so I was again lingering with death: The wages of sin is death. How old-fashioned it all was.

I'd read all about that, but now, as it arose in my mind, it still took me by surprise. The triumph of being alive became an amalgam producing a sense of confusion and pain. You are alive, others are not. One could live in this thought as in a house. But I was ashamed even before the dead, because I had it better than they did.

At ten-thirty I was assailed by the feeling that even after this eventful day something else might happen. I became impatient and nervous, a very common condition with leptosomes; the pyknic type is immune to this sort of tension. To put a stop to this torturous condition, I decided to go out again in order to hasten the arrival of whatever event, as I believed, was awaiting me. I would take my stick with me.

When you're rich, you face the problem of free will with immeasurably greater strength since you're free of many dependencies that otherwise govern your life, and so you're constantly having to make choices.

A full moon loomed over the separating woods as I left House One. As I got used to its cold light, I became aware that I was dressed too lightly. I rubbed my hands against the cold: a gesture of my father.

Across the street, under a streetlight, a figure lingered. The streetlight was out, so I couldn't see her face. She stood there like someone hesitating, someone who wants something but doesn't know if she really wants it.

Britta?

27

Then she made up her mind and walked over to me.

She had a bottle of champagne in her hand.

She asked whether I noticed anything special about her.

She smiled, and I was about to say no when I spotted it.

Isn't it beautiful? Say it's beautiful!

I knew how happy it makes a young person to get something they want, and agreed with her.

She suggested we go up and drink a toast. She wanted to return the favor for the champagne the other day.

It was a girl different from her usual self who ran up the steps, and I didn't know if it was her intention to get me all aroused with her movements.

Light the candle, like the other evening.

Here's a stick a boy meant to use to beat me over the head today, I said.

She took the stick and looked at the initials. Yeah, this belongs to Jacko's younger brother.

She drank and handed me the cup.

I told her that I found out today that my father had died.

She said she was sorry and asked if she should go.

No, I answered and drank. I told her to stay here and console me.

So how should she console me?

That was just a stupid joke, I answered and told her how much like a beauty-pageant queen she looked. My father, I continued, was a private man who kept to himself, a contented, perhaps even happy man. He rose up the ranks at work. But whenever he thought about his family's history, his pride in his ancestors was diluted by melancholy over the overall decline of the clan.

While I sat there remembering my father, Britta had gotten undressed and sat down on my lap naked. I'd often seen this in movies and dreams. Now you've got to pour champagne over her breasts and lick it up, I thought.

How banal was that now! No, I wasn't doing it.

Then I touched her breast anyway.

For a second I had to think of my wealth.

Considering the gap in age and our completely different lives, I hadn't counted on bringing the girl to climax; yet I managed it almost playfully. Shortly before returning to my default state of indifference, I watched her open her mouth and saw her teeth. No one would ever have guessed that a gaping hole had once been there.

I now had everything I needed in the settlement.

We were freezing, I pulled the bed covers over us.

If she were to ask me now who I was and what my intentions were, in this state of bliss I would reveal everything to her.

She said Armbruster had lent her the rest of the money.

It was obvious that she really didn't want to get into it.

After all, had we not just lain naked next to one another, forever captured by the moment?

Don't say a word!

The bed was too narrow for the two of us and I lay my arm around her shoulder so it wouldn't be in the way.

I'll be leaving the settlement.

Who just said that?

I wanted to fall in love with you. But it didn't work out.

That's her voice, I thought.

I'd become sad. Why do you feel so wounded? I asked myself sardonically. You yourself aren't capable of loving her either!

Still, it was good with you.

Yeah, I thought so too, I told her. The city sprang to mind, my father's death, my mother, the mayor's wife, Gesellius, who hated me—everything I wanted to forget.

So it all comes down to goodbye? I asked her and laughed.

Yes. But not for a few days.

She stroked me, aroused me; I wanted to resist, to preserve my grief. Finally, I gave in.

During the night, she got up, unable to sleep on account of the narrow bed, and went home to House Thirteen.

28

Now that I could afford individualism, it no longer struck me as worth pursuing. I took leave of my earlier persona, ideal the dandy. An aesthetic lifestyle is no more than laborious ostentation. It seemed to me now superfluous to craft an image of myself. Leading a beautiful life—for this, it was not necessary that life satisfy aesthetic norms, rather it was enough for freedom to take wing in any direction one liked.

With such thoughts on my mind, I called my mother in the morning. I told her I had just now learned of my father's death, that I was in America and so couldn't get back till next week.

He'd died very quickly, and that's the way she would like to die, my mother answered in her typically high voice—when she lies, she makes the mistake of speaking in a deeper voice to make the lie sound believable. He had done the ten-o'clock tour, an exclusively Japanese tour, dismissed the group and dropped dead on the spot. He was still holding the tip money in his hand. Yes, she was sad, but, even more, unhinged.

I had to hang up, I told her; I was on a plane to New York and had to turn off my cell phone, the directive to that effect having just flashed above me. I said I'd fly back from New York and come straight home to her.

She asked if I was doing well.

It did me good to hear my mother's voice, and when I stepped out into the young morning, with the sun shining and me not freezing despite my thin clothing, I felt oddly consoled over the course of the world. The settlement I had to cross through on my way to the woods struck me as the place on earth where I would've preferred to stay forever—this, despite its dreary houses, despite the old people hobbling along on their canes, despite the truant pupils standing around and smoking at their hangouts.

I had taken my stick with me for self-defense purposes in case I should get involved in another incident. As I passed House Thirteen, I saw two truant kids standing there smoking, and I called to them from a distance asking whether they were interested in the gift of a stick. That's when I saw that one of the two was my attacker, the stick's previous owner. Even so, I dropped the stick and went on my way calmly.

The kiosk appeared; it was still closed.

In the woods, I thought about how I might make my attic even more austere, more spartan, but came to no conclusions. Deeper in the woods, I heard a hammering, and, following the sound, I came upon a clearing where years ago the wurst stand had stood. Builders were sawing and hammering there, and when I enquired of one of them, he told me that the old wurst stand had indeed been torn down but that a new one bearing the old name would be constructed on the very site. In a long struggle with the forest authority, a citizens' action group had finally compelled this resurrection.

I left the construction site behind me and felt like risking another look at the city. As I did so, I thought about this and that, just not about my wealth. One thing in particular had become clear to me since coming into this inheritance: that too frequent, too long, too intense a dwelling on the money would, in the long run, unhinge my brain.

The city lay before me, harmless and threatening as ever.

At lunchtime I heated up a can of Armbruster's ravioli. After that, I spent the torturous afternoon reading in my book and looking at the disk.

That evening I went out again, to Armbruster's, to shop. The grocer said not a word about the girl's tooth, nor did he comment on my purchases as usual—he was lost in thought and remained mute with an occasional sigh.

Later on, as I'd hoped but no longer expected, Britta showed up. She had champagne with her.

Your face, I said, you look like a totally new person.

Even yesterday she already had this new look, she said.

Perhaps because we knew we'd soon be parting and not seeing each other again, we were a little contemptuous of each other. She had brought two glasses with her, two "goblets," like the ones in TV series from which a man and a woman sip champagne.

We managed the love-making itself very well; I almost felt shame over it. Indeed, I caught myself believing I was a good lover though well aware that was not the case.

She said she now had the kiosk at the market place.

I'd sat down on the chair, while she lay on the bed too narrow for two, and listened to her.

She said a new era was dawning for her; all at once she felt the initiative to care about a career, maybe to undertake an apprenticeship.

But, since I'd never have to work again, this conversation struck me as odd. It was as if I didn't understand what it meant, all these words: "work," "training," "career."

I told her it was a shame she would be leaving the area, that she and Armbruster were very important to me, and that I had no intention of quitting the settlement.

I saw my book lying on the table, and, hoping to win her admiration, I picked it up and started reading aloud from it. Much of it she knew, occasionally she laughed at the children's notions about the propagation of the race. After three or four pieces her interest waned.

I told her I had collected all these sayings, getting some of them straight from the children. My aim was to snatch them from the jaws of oblivion.

Was there money to be made from them?

I shook my head. I told her if she left, I'd have only Armbruster.

Was she sleeping? Had she heard me?

Armbruster might be leaving too, she said.

Suddenly I felt abandoned; I also noticed that I was freezing and turned on the space heater.

She got dressed. I watched her as she did and found her beautiful.

I'll come twice more, then no more, she said at the door.

I walked over to her and kissed her.

She asked me if I was one of the rich ones who lived incognito here in Backofen.

I hesitated. Then I wanted to tell all. But she was already gone.

29

The next evening Britta didn't show up.

I had eaten lunch at the kiosk, and she hadn't been there either, and although the weather was brilliant, it became clear to me just how delicate the glow and the equilibrium of the quarter were. I ate at a bar table, and suddenly I had an experience such as I'd had in the past: The thing my mother told me about yesterday on the phone did a repeat performance in my head: I saw my father standing in front of the Grissmann House, scarcely taller than the Japanese surrounding him. He was smiling. Then he emitted a soft cry (my mother hadn't said anything about this), his left hand holding the money in a clenched fist as he fell to the ground.

Never would he learn of my wealth.

To console myself over the girl's absence, I read again that evening in the book with the children's verses, and recalled a sentence Krautmann had once let drop in a lecture about intersubjectivity: You will never know how his beer tastes to the construction worker …

The next evening, when again she didn't show, I went to Armbruster's basement store.

Ah, he said, when he saw me, ah, and I braced for bad tidings.

I told him I'd heard that he too had helped Britta out with money.

Yes, the philosopher answered tersely. Did I want champagne again?

No, I answered. Tomorrow Britta was to leave the settlement forever, I told him, and I wouldn't see her again. So I wasn't in the mood for champagne. I said she meant to visit me today and yesterday, but hadn't done it. I told him to give me a bottle of red wine, but a good one. I'd use it to drown my melancholy.

The girl had been in the surgical ward since yesterday, and that was the reason she didn't come, Armbruster replied, putting a bottle down in front of me.

I wanted to ask the grocer if he didn't know of another, similar, girl here in the settlement, someone who could replace Britta's role with me, since I wanted to stay here. But then I thought better of it.

Jacko?

He said he didn't know. Could even have been the father. He added she was missing two front teeth now, so our mission had been in vain. "I have no new money for her," he concluded with a sneer."

Small potatoes, I wanted to shout, no problem, the money is there!

What's with the snarky tone, Armbruster?

Not meant for me, he said, this scorn was directed at fate. For neither this small blow of fate nor the greater one in the offing would deter him from his attitude of acceptance.

Maybe now she'll come back to the settlement, the grocer continued; that would certainly be fine with me.

Tomorrow I'll visit her, I said.

I had turned around, about to leave the store; any second now my steps would reverberate in the basement hallway; then came the autumnal night air—when Armbruster called after me:

Are you rich beyond measure?

I acted as though I hadn't heard the question, actually not being sure I hadn't imagined it, and stepped outside.

You will—cold fog pushed into the settlement from the separating woods—stay here as long as it suits you.

At home I sat drinking Armbruster's red wine when suddenly—it was already late—I caught myself comparing Armbruster with Morler and Helena with Britta and wondering whom I would prefer if I had to choose. But then I was rich and a rich man has no need to choose, since he can have anything. Such considerations bothered me. I pushed them aside, thought about nothing and continued to drink.

30

Yesterday was an eventful day. Just think, at its end I may have performed an heroic deed!

I had taken the bus into town with the intention of seeing my mother. Then, at the bus station, all the lies I had dished up to her came into my head: superfluous lies I would've had to explain if I visited her this week. Good, I thought, lets go clothes-shopping first, maybe shoes, then up to the castle. From there you have a fabulous view on a beautiful Fall day.

At ten a.m., the stores opened and I stepped into Frauendiener's. An old-fashioned bell tinkled and old Frauendiener himself shuffled out towards me from the back of the store.

I told him I was the son of a caretaker and needed new clothing.

Frauendiener is small and fragile, an elfin old man with a still-smooth face and a full head of gray hair. He seems impervious to age; right to the grave, I thought, he'll look the way he does now.

So, the son of a caretaker, he repeated pensively, and now you want to look like a rich man?

He reached for a seemingly unremarkable suit. When I tried it on, I saw that he was right: Yes, that's the way I wanted to look.

Now I needed something else, something that would make me look younger, youthful, savage even.

That too Frauendiener can supply, a leather jacket, black leather pants, all of the finest quality, finest workmanship, and yet having the effect of alarming me before my own image in the mirror.

I don't know you, said the clothier as he put down the appropriate shoes, but have you perhaps gotten rich in foreign lands, returned home after a long absence and now want to avenge yourself on your hometown?

We laughed together over this romantic nonsense.

I paid, left my purchases there for the time being and exited the shop.

I needed new money.

You again? Gesellius called out to me in greeting.

I need fresh money, I answered.

He didn't mean that the way it came out, said Gesellius as he counted out the bills.

He asked who was now giving the tours of the Grissmann House, now that my father had passed.

Don't you know? Haven't you been to your mother's yet?

No, I meant to see her today, I said, uncertain whether I was lying.

Your mother's doing it now.

During this dialog I became aware of the garish elegance with which the bank director's office had been appointed. Gesellius, I thought, you used to have style.

Do you want to know the good deed I have in mind?

Gesellius just shakes his head and waits for me to leave.

He hopes to get rid of me with some good news.

He tells me he has arranged it so that only he and no other associate is to know of my wealth.

It's nice of you to visit, says Britta.

Behind the bandages her face is hardly recognizable.

She begins to cry but no doubt finds it painful and stops.

It's a three-bed room, the other two beds are empty.

She holds her hand in front of her mouth and says in a voice I've never heard her use, doubtless a result of her injuries: Everything's for shit now.

I tell her I've brought her flowers, purchased in the lobby downstairs.

Everything'll be all right, I say. And want to ask who beat her up, but I skip it. Instead, I ask her if she's in pain.

She's been given painkillers, she answers in her ghostly voice.

It's afternoon, the time when I am weak and helpless vis-a-vis the world, I'm hungry since I haven't had lunch yet, an autumn sun shines on Britta's bed, and I want to put all this quickly behind me now, pick up my new clothes and shoes and get back to the attic. Or go to Armbruster's and discuss the baseness of the world with him, or even its potential splendor.

Here, I say, for you. You don't have to go back to the settlement. Just take it. It might be hot, I say laughing.

A sentence like that is a cue to exit, and I leave the clinic, happy that school is out and I am free.

How easy I find farewells these days!

On to the Deutsches Haus. Let me hide there from the afternoon.

Never would I know how my father liked the schnitzel; that makes me nostalgic.

For now, though, I want to take a walk by the river. That's helped me before.

It was three in the afternoon. I walked downstream along the boardwalk heading for the dam. The sun shone on the water, a warm, light wind caused the river to shimmer. I was no one.

After I'd walked for a while, the dam came into view.

To postpone my arrival, I sat down on one of the benches on the bank.

The river becomes wider before the dam but still flows fast. The river dazzled me.

Something was about to happen.

The light danced upon the water and I screwed up my eyes. Jewels, diamonds, precious stones.

Something's about to happen, I thought.

There wasn't a soul in sight.

Now! I thought, now!

Something was floating in the water.

I'd already taken my jacket off. Now just shoes and sweater. My pants I kept on.

Since my youth I've been a good swimmer.

I looked around to see if there wasn't a life preserver somewhere near the banks. There wasn't.

The river's shimmer led me to think the water was warm. The cold took my breath away. I dove in and headed for the driftwood. The current pulled at me, there wasn't a sound. Silently the water drove me towards the dam. You're going to die now and you didn't call on your mother. That thought made the water colder, the current stronger. Don't be stupid, I thought, think about something else. Children's verses came to me. Why did I go into the water? Don't think about it! Calmly I swam in a warm lake.

How easily I handled partings! Including this one right now from myself. Anyway, I began to play games, to slow things down.

I swam with long, powerful strokes.

I wasn't getting any closer to my goal. The punchline of a joke occurred to me, one I'd heard a long time ago, and I could feel myself smile as I swam. I could no longer see the clump bundle??, too blinded by the precious stones. Turning around briefly, I saw my clothes lying on the bench on the bank, much closer to me then the driftwood. Something is about to happen. I can still get to my clothes. Nobody'll see that you're not rescuing the child. Who knows, it might already be dead. During all this I'd made progress swimming.

My money was in my jacket.

God, I thought, haven't people always drowned here?

I listened for a voice deep within to tell me whether my foot was about to cramp up. Because then it's all over, I thought with satisfaction.

Some water seeped into my mouth.

Death would loosen all bonds for me: I wouldn't have needed my wealth at all.

Bits and pieces from my past passed through my mind, the beautiful time in America when the old man died; but other things too, movies I'd seen. Tarzan's roar in an old black-and-white film. Nobody swam as well as Tarzan. In the jungle the water was warm. Playfully easy, paying no mind to the crocodiles, Tarzan sped ahead: water his element. In my mind's eye, I saw the headlines, the photos, the film: Tarzan saving the child from drowning.

I'd reached my goal. Now the other bank was closer.

I grabbed the little body and brought it to land without difficulty. How light it was!

It was a girl, maybe five years old. I laid her on the lawn. On the other side of the river, I saw my pile of clothes on the bench.

As I began resuscitation efforts, you could hear the first siren.

Now your mother'll find out you're here and didn't look her up right away.

I pressed both hands against the tiny ribcage. How easily I could crush the girl's ribs! Maybe she was already dead. If she came alive, she'd have Tarzan to thank for her life, not me.

She opened her eyes. One was green, the other brown.

Eyes of green are serpentine.

I trembled with cold.

31

Firefighters and paramedics were all around me, police too. There was no escape. They took the girl from me and placed her in the ambulance.

Someone handed me a blanket and asked me questions. The first rubberneckers crowded in. An old woman had seen everything and told the story over and over. How the child fell into the water, how I got into the water, how the child drifted to the dam, how I swam to it, how the child fell into the water, how she called the fire department, how she saw everything and called the fire department …

Enough! I barked at her.

She shut up in astonishment, then turned once again to the bystanders, this time telling in a softer voice: how the child fell into the river, how she saw it, how I'd taken my clothes off and gotten into the river, how I reached the child and brought it to the bank, how she'd seen it all and called the fire department …

You have no right, I thought, to forbid the woman to speak.

There was an ambulance there for me too and they advised me to lie down on the gurney.

I told the police there was a lot of money in my jacket and could they please drive me to my clothes on the other side of the river.

In the police car, I laid the blanket under me to avoid wetting the seat with my pants.

When they had me get out, they asked for my personal effects.

I've got money here, I said, taking it out of my jacket. How much would you take to let me remain anonymous? I've got money here, I repeated, holding bills in both hands to give them to both of them.

No, said the older man finally, I was to show my ID on the spot, plus they would be checking to see if I was on any wanted lists.

I was freezing. I thought of Tarzan and how he had saved the girl.

You've already been photographed, said the young man, giving me back my ID. He said there would be no getting around a report in the newspapers.

I'd like to be alone now, I said. They should call me a taxi. The two of them stood there wavering, then they made a phone call and took off.

There was no one left on the opposite shore. Only the old woman still stood there, surrounded by four people—correction, now only three. At one point she pointed over at me, and the gazes of her listeners followed her outstretched hand. I couldn't see what they might be thinking, only the telephones in their hands with which they photographed me.

The taxi arrived; the driver, an older man, already knew everything.

I told him I was tired and wet, and didn't want to hear anything about myself or my actions. He was simply to take me to the Backofen Settlement.

No one falls into the same river twice.

At home I lay down on the bed, though it was still afternoon, and fell into a heavy sleep.

I would often wonder in those days, when all possibilities were open to me, whether a bad life would not be preferable to a good one that ended in mere tedium.

The next day I visited my mother.

I called on her in the evening, an hour after she'd closed the Grissmann House, wanting to give her time to rest up from her new job.

When I rang, she opened the apartment door with a tired movement, as though expecting nothing pleasant from this unexpected visit. Probably because she wasn't counting on seeing me, she didn't immediately recognize me; then she flung her arms around my neck and pressed me to herself with an intensity that surprised me. She seemed to be quite starving for corporeal closeness.

Here, I said, freeing myself and handing her the flowers, the chocolates and the bottle of wine. All of it I'd bought at Armbruster's.

Finally you're here.

Yes, I answered. She'd not grown smaller with time and was still taller than her husband had been. It occurred to me that he was dead.

She said she was just having supper and that I should keep her company, then it would be like old times.

Again she wanted to embrace me, but then thought better of it.

She asked if I'd be staying in the city for a while. There had been a picture in the newspaper, and although it was very blurry, the man in it looked like me. More his attitude than his appearance, vague and unassertive, the facial expression as if asking little of life.

Let's talk about it over dinner, I said. Is there herring from the can, in red sauce?

We sat at the kitchen table with the radio playing low. We ate in silence, but she examined me again and again. I ate the herring, hated dish of my youth. It was outstanding.

It's time for you to tell me, I said, what a shame it is that I didn't become a professor. That would make me feel completely at home. Want to talk about Papa?

Tomorrow, she answered.

We repaired to the living room for wine. I had to marvel at my parents' taste: With scant means they had so appointed the small room that one immediately recognized its congruence with the arrangement of the Grissmann House.

Here's the man, said my mother, handing me the newspaper. He saved a little girl's life. How proud she would be if it had been me. Saving a life, a child's life no less—there would be nothing greater one could achieve in life.

I said nothing. I was enjoying a sense of well-being in my mother's company; just sitting here drinking a glass of wine let me forget the rest of the world. In this moment, in this Grissmann dollhouse, everything I wished from life seemed to me to be contained.

Yes, I thought so too, I said, when I noticed she was expecting an answer.

Time passed.

Speak up now, I urged myself. If you put it off, it'll get harder and harder, in the end even impossible.

She asked when I'd returned from America.

This morning, I answered. And by the way, I became rich over there.

It grew dark outside, and my mother turned on the chandelier, a replica of the one in the museum, a present from my father. Its light was too bright for the small room.

Yes, yes, the old woman answered. Old woman? Where did I get that? Yes, my mother was old in that merciless light. Soon I'd be old too. Time marches on regardless.

What a shame that you didn't become a professor! You had the makings.

I nodded. How many times had I heard that! Now it no longer had a purchase on me. And a most appealing thought added even more to my well-being: You will take over your father's post. That's how you'll spend your life, not as a hero or a rich man.

She had to go to bed now, my mother said finally. The job at the Grissmann House wore her out. I shouldn't tell anyone, but the work was no fun. If I wanted, she could put fresh linen on the bed in the children's room.

I'd be spending the night in the attic, I answered. But she should let me sit here for a while, even as she slept, and finish my wine.

I heard her go into the bathroom, then into the bedroom.

My mother slept. I sat in the living room and saw the Solitaire cards on the table. I picked them up and dealt out her favorite Solitaire game, "Harp." It was night and very quiet.

Krautmann, I thought, if I could describe this scene and the feelings it evoked in me—it would come very close to an idea of home.

32

My gait has changed. Like every morning, I had roamed through the settlement, then a little through the forest, and when I came out of the forest, on my way to Armbruster's, I noticed that I was keeping myself more upright than usual; then, having been struck by the first signs, I became aware that I was walking more slowly and, without being conscious of it up to then, rolling my shoulders and hips more, as sailors and boxers do.

I tried to suppress this new gait, tried to remember how I had walked as a student and, subsequently, as a traveling speaker—like the drifter I had been in recent years: somewhat stooped, carelessly dragging my feet, arms dangling, head set back with annoying insolence. For a while it worked. But no sooner did my attention lapse than I would fall again into the new way of walking.

I have to study that, I thought, as I arrived at Armbruster's.

I was not immediately served as a young man stood in front of me wanting to buy a bottle of beer.

I wanted to alert Armbruster to the fact that the youth was a minor, but then decided not to. It was the same fellow who had come at me with the stick. We recognized each other, skipped the greeting and he quickly picked up his bottle and left the basement.

So then, said Armbruster in lieu of a greeting.

I'd intended to chew the fat with Armbruster; my purchases were simply a pretext for this; but now he had infected me with his seriousness—indeed, his dismay.

What's up, Armbruster? I exclaimed with a laugh; so then, so then, what's that supposed to mean?

He'd watched me, he answered, as I walked towards him in the basement hallway, and something about me tipped him off to it.

My gait?

He didn't respond to that.

So it's you after all, the man in the newspaper.

And if it is?

We don't want any attention brought to the quarter, he replied.

No, I said, but what man, what did he do? I told him I hadn't read the paper.

Armbruster shook his head, and I felt ashamed of my lies.

What he said made me uneasy, but even more his dejection, and it wasn't until I recalled to consciousness that I was free to go anywhere I wanted that the anxiety that had gripped me let loose.

It might be this store will not be around for much longer.

Aren't people spending enough?

I told him I was buying things I had no need for, but this failed to cheer him up. Totally withdrawn, he put everything in front of me; then he noticed my good intentions and smiled.

As I was leaving, he said there was an ideal place for each of us. And his might just be prison.

No one can simply live wherever he wants to. Even if he's rich. At some point I would have to leave the settlement. Maybe I'd move to the city, or to my mother's. Or to America.

As I approached House One with my groceries, I saw two women and a man standing by the door. Maybe it was the sight of these three people that evoked in me thoughts of staying and leaving. But Armbruster's philosophical reflections about the ideal place may also have played a part.

It was a couple in their mid-thirties, elegantly yet unremarkably dressed—a fact making them all the more striking here in the settlement—and a younger woman in a fashionable leather jacket.

That's him.

They made way so that I could get to the entrance and unlock it.

We want to thank you, the man said.

I told him I had no time.

We're the parents, said his partner.

The younger woman was carrying a camera and took pictures. That's when I discovered some writing attached to the house wall, new and in red.

Here live rich people. And under that, a bit smaller, in black: House One! We know you!

The photographer said she was from the newspaper and these were the parents of little Sophia. They wanted to thank me. They didn't know who I was or where I lived and her newspaper found out the information for her from the police.

Cut that out! I bellowed.

But she just kept photographing me. From a few meters away bystanders began to observe us. The boy with the stick was among them. I unlocked the door and let the three of them into the hallway, to escape the gaze of the curious.

Please don't take it amiss, I said, turning to the couple, but I do not wish to be associated with the action I took. That would be a burden.

I looked into the face, first of the woman, then of the man, and, though it was day, even turned on the stairway light: The woman had brown eyes, the man green.

The woman said they were well off and wanted to reward me for my deed, even if no reward in the world was adequate to it.

Almost at the same time, the journalist asked me what it meant to me to have saved a human life.

From outside you could hear the bystanders calling out something; it was a loud, incomprehensible murmuring.

What are they shouting? the journalist asked. What about the rich?

Tarzan, I thought, Tarzan would have been happy and satisfied with his deed. With me it was not so simple.

Yes, I answered, not sure I'd be able to find the right words, it was great fun to save a child from drowning.

As I spoke, you could hear the loud shattering of a pane of glass. The noise devoured my words, and even the journalist's mic probably did not pick them up. I opened the front door and looked out. There was no one in sight.

You don't need to live here, said the child's mother, we can make it possible for you to move to town.

Get lost, beat it! I shouted.

They acted as if they hadn't heard me right; then the father slipped his calling card into my grocery bag.

I climbed the stairs. Up to the third floor I could still hear them talking it over. Then I no longer heard them, and forgot about them.

Armbruster, I thought, what's up with you?

For a few days I had peace.

33

I'll have Morler come. I want his assurance that nothing's changed. That they're not going to drive me out of the settlement, and that nothing's going to happen to Armbruster.

I'd made myself some coffee and drank it out of the tin cup I'd just purchased at the grocery store; the sensation of tin on my lips and teeth reminded me of a campfire, of the life of a cowboy. Yes, I expected Morler to handle the situation in the settlement and any problems having to do with the city.

It was three p.m. when I had this idea. At six, in order to get over a slight indisposition, I took the bus into the city to eat. For the occasion, I put on my new clothes, which had meanwhile been delivered.

Except for me the bus was empty. If it were up to me, it could stay that way forever. I still hadn't been to my father's grave. I wandered through the city and thought of the many times I'd hated it. Everything here, I thought, the city, the settlement, you yourself, is only temporary; only the Grissmann House is eternal.

I decided on the Krone Restaurant. Once, shortly before his disappearance, Krautmann had invited us there. But dark intimations about his and our future had killed the appetites of us assistants.

I was alone in the place. Only at one table behind a column were there other guests, whom I could hear but not see. It reminded me of another visit to a restaurant, a long time ago in Berlin, before I'd become rich. How many years ago was that? Only three weeks ago. Maybe rich people go by a different sense of time.

The waiter brought the menu. He was a muscular fellow with oily, slicked-back hair and gave the appearance of someone brought in from the wrestling mat and stuffed into a waiter's jacket.

Here, he said, adding in a whisper that the mayor was sitting behind the column and also just about to dine.

The mayor was not alone. Someone was with him, they were conversing.

There sat the man my wife was now living with. A slanted fall sun shone through the window; from outside you could hear the pedestrian traffic crossing the bridge. I was at peace with myself.

Even his gait has changed, said a voice from behind the column. It sounded worried. Never would it occur to the mayor to sound worried.

In response, the booming, devil-may-care voice of the mayor rang out. One might have supposed a giant behind this laugh.

And now, the first voice continued, annoyed by the other's indifference, he's even a hero to boot!

Yes, agreed the mayor in his full, smarmy, menacing voice. That's something he would never have thought the wretch capable of. He would love to have performed that act of derring-do himself. What a shame he wasn't there on the spot!

My appetizer came. And as I continued to listen to the conversation, I brooded over the question why I had been so happy yesterday in my mother's living room.

Someone was telling the mayor he should also rein in his sex drive, especially so close to an election; there were haters afoot who could exploit that politically.

You think so? the mayor answered, again erupting into his carefree laugh.

This laughter, I thought, is his sharpest weapon. It promises to solve all the city's problems.

Again I recalled now that my wife during our separation had praised the mayor as a tireless lover, and how I, when she said that, had wished I were an old man, an ancient man, someone who had nothing more to do with all that.

Did he really have to keep up that damned laughing, exclaimed the first man in annoyance.

Now I recognized the voice: Gesellius was sitting there, talking with the mayor about the latter's political future.

Be wary of him, he's become powerful and may very well exact his revenge!

Good, replied the mayor, adding that he would invite the agitator to city hall and honor him as a lifesaver.

The waiter walked past me carrying two silver platters under two silver thermal covers. They had to be holding capons, the house specialty. (I had ordered the same thing myself.)

I could hear the men eating. And, as the waiter returned to the serving counter and came back in shortly thereafter with another platter, I thought he was going to serve me my entrée. But again he disappeared behind the column.

I stood up and walked over to them. The big, lanky mayor with his red hair, Gesellius in a snakeskin jacket, and between them a third person, who up to now had been silent.

So she'd fallen into the mayor's hands after all!

Britta was wearing an evening dress. The sight of her round, naked shoulders caused my heart to contract. Her teeth were luminous. Only if you looked closely could you see the blue facial blemishes covered by makeup.

So you've fallen into Bergius' hands, have you! I repeated.

Bergius composed himself quickly, and without interrupting what he was doing—he was carving the girl's capon, cutting the meat into small bits and placing them on her plate—he smiled at me. Before he went into politics, Bergius had been a Latin teacher. We pupils adored him.

Gesellius had gotten up from his seat, ready to lunge at me if I got physical.

I just wanted to live in the Backofen Settlement a little longer, nothing more than that, I said.

Britta signaled to me not to mention the business about her teeth, and, as a sign of agreement, I winked at her.

Sit down, Gesellius, the mayor shouted laughing, you know what a strongman I am, I don't age, and, should Georg lay hands on me, I would make short work of him. Come, Georg, join us!

He gestured to the waiter to set another place.

My meal came, and for a while we ate capon in silence.

When you unexpectedly become rich, you have to learn everything all over again, all behavior towards yourself and others. Just as if you'd lost the use of language and had to acquire it anew.

Then the cook
Alone it took,
And stuck it in the oven nook.

said Bergius finally. Do you know that one, Britta? The kids don't circulate it anymore. Georg wanted to rescue it.

Then Bergius proposed that everyone at the table predict his or her own future.

One thing you should know ahead of time, the mayor went on, your wife knows about Britta—as about all the others. She loves me anyway, as I do her.

I wanted to respond to my Latin teacher, but Britta beat me to it.

Bergius will jilt me, the girl said. Then she would move to a big city, do an apprenticeship and experience adventures.

We'd finished our dinners. I started to comment on Britta's prophecy, but Bergius indicated to me that that was beside the point.

How young he had stayed! He looked like an old pupil. As for us, by contrast, Gesellius and me, who had sat in his class, every sign of youth had vanished.

You'll win the election, Gesellius declared, and he would personally see to it that no agitator prevented it!

Yes, I'll win the election, Bergius repeated.

Again he laughed. And it was precisely this laugh with which he had given out the worst grades in class. But you mustn't stoop to measuring yourself against him, I thought. Conceivably, compared to you, the mayor is a dwarf.

They were looking at me; it was my turn.

Seduced by the frivolity of the game, I said I would follow in my father's footsteps and assume his position as caretaker, custodian, tour guide, but then added: that is, if I, wretch though I be, do not take my revenge on you, Bergius.

We took leave of each other in good spirits.

The mayor had grabbed the check. For a moment we stood around in front of the place; the cool of autumn was in the air and we enjoyed sensing how our bodies, fortified with the best cuisine, mastered the chill. For a moment, we were a community.

He had things to do, the mayor told Britta. He wouldn't be able to take her home today.

And so each of us went his own way.

Later I was alone in my attic. I opened the window. A full moon was poised above the separating forest and shone in on me. The loneliness was gone. Already my mind was empty of thoughts. Correction: I thought of the night wind, which calmly entered and cooly caressed my face.

In the Grissmann House

34

Perhaps it was time to acquaint myself with the particulars of my wealth. But I feared for my newly won freedom. Particularity always hems one in, robs one of possibilities, everything one does necessarily excludes other deeds one might have performed. And so I sensed how the city began to shape me and box me in, in consequence of the notoriety of my rescue, this despite my true secret's never having been exposed. How could the "child rescuer from Wennfelder Garten" prowl the streets at night caterwauling, as I so used to enjoy doing as a student? In Backofen glasses would clink when in the morning I'd stroll past the clusters of beer drinkers at the kiosk: That's the one who saved little Sophia. But I could tell they didn't love me for that, but rather that they felt some vague anxiety towards me.

Let the mayor, I would think in such moments, let Bergius claim it was he who saved the girl. I'd have been fine with that.

Morler arrived today.

He strikes me as bigger than back then; he stands before me, smiling, with sparkling white teeth—like someone who doesn't need me. A baldy with bursting vitality. Maybe, I think, you're not even close to being a match for him.

Is it you, Morler? I ask, as he stands on the threshold making ready to come in.

You asked me for help. Here I am.

His presence filled the entire attic; the place was almost bursting at the seams.

What's this?! he shouted in my face after taking a quick look around my abode, what, is this how a rich man lives?

He was outraged, as if he'd been deceived, as if the world must always lie and intentionally overcomplicate everything. But then he broke out into a resounding laughter.

So this is how you live, huh!

He raised his forefinger threateningly. You'd be amazed at what I know! the gesture seemed to mean.

Now, however, I was to describe my situation to him. Every problem had a solution.

Had I not known him from earlier, I would've thought it was a stranger standing before me: The detective was brimming with optimism and vitality.

I described my situation and asked for his advice. Alas! I added parenthetically before he could answer. I told him I had booked him at the Krone for the length of his stay; there, in my place and at my expense, he was free to lead the life of a rich man. But he must not let this freedom cause him to neglect his duties.

Didn't I wish to inquire about his situation, Morler exclaimed instead of replying. For in fact his life was outstanding, he insisted.

His extremely good mood had something intimidating about it. How glad I would've been to be rid of this maniac again!

The offer appealed to him, the detective continued. It had always been his wish to lead the life of a rich man. By the way, he added, he had another reason for wanting to thank me.

His voice became confidential.

It was for my don't-give-a-shit attitude towards the world. He'd adopted it for himself. Now once again life was fun for him, even if he'd suffered at times from his exaggerated euphoria. Now he could work better than ever. But now off to the hotel! If I wanted, I could join him for dinner. I should be there in two hours.

That last matter Morler had mentioned in an imperious tone of voice, a tone that did not sit well with me. But then I thought, what difference did it make if the detective were to rob me of decisions! After all, if money no longer played a roll in making decisions, then the number of possible decisions was legion, and all assistance gratefully accepted.

In the Hotel Krone, Morler has taken the prince suite. It used to be called the Grissmann suite, after an ancestor of mine, a mayor of the city during the Thirty Years War. I give the detective free rein; indeed, it tickles me to see how he wastes my money.

When I entered the restaurant two hours later, Morler was already sitting at the table behind the column where two days earlier the mayor had sat.

This was the mayor's table, Morler called out to me—however, he had secured it anyway. With a flourishing gesture, he pointed to the seat opposite him and I sat down.

Morler had already ordered, and had also, as he put it, taken the liberty of ordering for me; capons were the dish of choice here.

Why not, I thought, the capon I'd eaten before was very good.

Just generally speaking, he went on, he could help me out on many fronts, if I wished him to and the pay was adequate.

Suddenly the conversation struck me as unpleasant; even the transformed Morler failed to jibe with my expectations, and I wondered whether I shouldn't just drop some cash in the detective's hand and ask him to leave the city. In spite of that I began to talk about myself. About the rush of satisfaction that often overcame me in the attic when I would gaze out the open window into the forest at night, drinking the philosopher Armbruster's red wine, humming to myself and thereby adding a second voice to the rustling of branches. Even the occasional nocturnal bellowing and whining of the drunkards on the children's playground could not disturb my peace of mind.

To my amazement, Morler immediately grasped what I was getting at, even giving the waiter who was about to serve the meal a signal to wait till I'd finished speaking. Yes, only now as I spoke of it, did I become aware of how good I had it in the Backofen Settlement.

When I finished, Morler said he envied me, even though he himself was carved from a completely different kind of wood, his new self included.

He looked off into some vague faraway place, smiled and gestured to the waiter to serve.

If you like, Georg, I can take charge of all your duties. That would leave me to carry on my attic lifestyle as long as I liked.

Yeah, I said, that sure sounds good to me.

We ate in silence. I was enjoying the capon and for a moment I thought I should eat here every day.

35

For the next three days, I wasn't in the city and met no one, not even Morler—he was to make no unsolicited contact with me, so I had stipulated. During this period, which struck me as endless, the lady journalist knocked on my door once. I opened but did not invite her in. She said, smiling, that her readers wanted to know more about me, and it seemed to me as though the young woman had purposely dressed to tantalize, with a short skirt and a T-shirt with plunging neckline. People don't forget a lifesaver that quickly, she said; also, I would be giving her career a boost if I granted her an interview.

The private detective Morler was staying at the Hotel Krone, I answered; she should look him up, he knew everything about me.

She did not respond to this, merely looking past me into the attic room where Helena's film was running on the TV screen. I turned my head. It was the part where the shoe salesgirl is placing shoes in the display window. No one was naked.

When she was gone, I called Morler to warn him: He could say anything he wanted about me, even tell lies if he felt like it. The only thing off limits was my wealth.

In a powerful voice trembling with high spirits, the detective gave his word.

Morler, I asked before hanging up, do you have a twin brother?

I finally visited my father's grave. It's the smallest among the Grissmann graves, even the dipso shoemaker who lost the house lies beneath a more stately stone.

Here, I said to him, I've brought you flowers.

It did me good to speak out loud to him; despite the beautiful afternoon, there were no other cemetery visitors to be seen.

I laid the flowers down, and my funeral wreath was so big that it covered the flowers already lying there.

Yeah, I said, I'm rich, even if with no effort on my part, purely through kinship and chance.

Not far away from the family graves may be found the gravestone of a poet whose work is dear to my heart; a few verses from a poem by him occurred to me. The theme is the course of one's life.

I thought I would briefly walk over to the poet's grave and after that go back to the settlement. Then I could tell Armbruster about it that afternoon. He too is an ardent admirer of this poet.

The bitter smell of boxwood hung in the air, and I shuffled through the colorful leaves lying on the paths. No one saw me as I kicked my way through the rustling leaves like a kid.

Two men are standing at the poet's grave.

I didn't want to share this moment of remembrance with anyone, so I turned around and left.

It was Bergius and Morler.

On this afternoon, I felt lonely again, this after a very long time. Armbruster has been arrested.

I had wanted to go to the store, still quite moved by my visit to the cemetery, but at the entrance to the house I found them coming towards me: Armbruster in handcuffs between two policemen. They wore trench coats, as in the movies, dour, serious-looking men who took care not to walk too fast for an old man.

Armbruster, what's the matter? I called out. But Armbruster just smiled and shook his head.

One of the cops looked at me and they stood still.

That's the man who saved the girl, he explained to his colleague. That was a fine thing you did.

For a moment I thought the policemen were giving off the smell of boxwood, but it was probably only a memory of my visit to the cemetery that morning.

I'll be writing an aesthetics, Georg! Armbruster suddenly shouted. And if it was me who fingered him, I had actually done him a favor. Still, he suspected the kid with the stick.

Now they were in a hurry, since the rubberneckers were crowding in, so they walked to their car and got in.

The afternoon sun appeared, which I so dreaded.

Yep, I thought, my time here is over. And, as the driver-side door again opened, and the second cop again got out, walked over to me and shook my hand, I again had the same thought: that I would move out of the settlement.

If you run for office, I'll vote for you.

The car took off, not fast, not slow, and I was no longer certain whether the policeman had really said that.

I stood there in the street for a while, as though waiting for the vacancy that Armbruster had left behind to fill up. But nothing happened, and I decided to go into the forest till the afternoon and my loneliness were done.

36

The wurst stand in the separating forest has been reopened. Whereas with its predecessor "Forest Bratwurst Stand" stood in carved wooden letters on the plank-sign over the door, now "Forest Bratwurst Shack" stands there. In his opening-day speech, the mayor called upon the people not to take this deviation from tradition too seriously, but rather to regard the shack as a "communal hub."

All of this I get from Morler, who manages to be everywhere and sees and hears everything.

He tells me that even the company that continues to supply the shack with wurst and meat has changed its name. It's now called "New Fleiko."

That's the sort of thing I don't want to hear, I tell Morler. Come on, Morler, I say, surely you've summoned me to this stand to tell me something of importance?

We're sitting on a rough-hewn wooden bench in front of the bratwurst stand. From here one has a beautiful view of the clearing, at the other end of which the forest resumes. A bit of fog residue wafts over the grass, smelling of bratwurst.

In the country lives a woodsman /
eats kids just like sausage goods, man

says Morler, indicating that he's also been very much concerned with me; it's a children's saying from my book:

In the far-off Chinese nation /
where I have no blood relation …

The dedication, he says, was a folk festival, everybody in a good mood and high spirits enjoying the free beer and free wurst; plus there was music. Pity, he adds after a brief pause during which his hands draw my attention, pity you weren't there.

Morler's hands are manicured, his big detective's hands trimmed to the max, even the two pinky fingers (finely shaved); with these Late Period hands he blathers on about folksy bonhomie and free beer. But, it occurs to me, these must be Bergius' words, here regurgitated to me by Morler. Then too, don't the mayor, and Gesellius, and the rescued girl's mother also have such manicured hands? And I picture to myself a secret society with this as its identifying sign. But then, I myself have, in my period of giving back-room lectures, often spent my last euro on a manicure. So as not to fall completely outside the community of civilized beings.

I had gotten lost in memories, and my gaze went out over the shreds of mist, until it came up against the forest in the distance.

If you don't run against Bergius, Morler added, the mayor is prepared to give you back your wife. This he learned from Bergius in the cemetery, where they had certainly seen me. Or did I think I was invisible?

He laughed.

I, however, did not really feel surprised by this as I expected nothing else.

Does she know I'm rich?

A delivery truck came into the clearing. Two men got out; I saw them clearly: the one cheerfully whistling, the other quiet, with the most measured movements such as mourners often make.

No, of course not! Morler said. Even Bergius didn't know a thing, though he may have had an inkling. Their friendship notwithstanding, Gesellius had not told him.

The sad sack opened the stand while the other man fetched the wurst from the delivery truck. There must have been hundreds.

Morler said a meeting had already been arranged between her and me. For today, in the Cafe Völter, at three. You know the cafe, don't you? He said he told Bergius he couldn't guarantee that I'd want Ingrid back. That meant I could make up my mind this afternoon without any hindrance.

Morler, I answered, who came up with the idea that I'd be standing for election? Please deny it!

Too late for that, he said, nobody would believe that now.

With these words he stood up and walked over to the stand where the roller blind was now being raised. The sad sack's upper body became visible, then his neck, then his head.

The first wurst is for me! Moerler shouted into the face of the man in the booth. The second for my friend Georg!

Don't be angry! he said, turning to me; you don't have to go there. She'll sit there for a while, realize you're not coming and go home.

I said I wouldn't hear of it. There was too much in the past that was still obscure, I thought, for me to occupy myself continually with the present and the future.

Morler, how much longer would you have run?

He turned red.

Morler, in America, what was going on? What were you feeling as you sped across that field? Know what I think? That you were happy on your little trek. Happier than ever before in your life. That for those four-hundred, five-hundred meters you were the happiest man on earth.

That is total bullshit, Morler shouts and laughs. But he did turn red, and before you know it he looks just the way he did then, deeply disappointed that he'd come to a standstill.

I shouldn't read anything into that, says the detective, looking me straight in the eye, as though I was the one who had run full-bore straight ahead on foreign soil, further and further into the foreign landscape, like someone just off the boat who wants to explore the unknown.

Oh, Morler! I want to answer, but he presses the cardboard container holding the minced wurst into my hand and tells me to eat. And Morler has already almost devoured his wurst, while I'm still taking my first bite and noticing that it doesn't taste good, and I stand up and toss the rest of my wurst into the trash bin, the way rich people do when something doesn't taste good; and, to placate the detective, who looks askance at me, I tell him that I'll be coming to Cafe Völter. And something else, Morler. Armbruster, the philosopher, has been arrested; look into it, will you?

I walked into the forest at a slow pace, and, without looking back, I knew that the three men followed me with their gaze and that not one of them understood me.

37

I got to the Cafe Völter too early. I like to be the second one there; then you can make an entrance with your gait, your wardrobe, the way you take off your coat or jacket. In this way you ground the meeting and set the tone.

None of that mattered to me this time.

Völter's is appointed with dark wooden furniture; lace see-through curtains cover the large windows that face the street and resemble display windows.

I sat down at a table by the window and looked out. How would Ingrid look now? I did not succeed in imagining her. Again and again a wedding photo got in the way. Like idiots, bride and groom smirk at the camera, next to us Krautmann as witness, looking as if he could already sense the future and was leading us into it anyway.

Britta came and asked for my order—no, there was only a vague similarity between the waitress and her; and, on closer look, none.

Bring me something, I said. I told her an acquaintance of mine had said I was to meet someone here, but that I now regarded that as a web of lies and was feeling uneasy in my own skin.

Something?

Everything else I'd said seemed to her to be of no interest.

At three, afternoon is still in the ascendency, and I felt keenly my own helplessness.

Coffee or beer, I answered.

A graybeard student barked at the waitress to bring him his bill and she left me.

I looked out at the street so familiar to me. The shop where I had bought my new clothes was on the other side. When the waitress returned with a glass of beer and a small pot of coffee, a quirk in my relationship to my wife came to mind again: that oftentimes I loved her more when I thought about her than when she was actually there.

A large, dark-haired woman of around forty had come in and was looking around. She spotted me immediately. Her green eyes emitted death rays. I thought of the years of our life together, and I didn't know if I'd be willing to endure her anew with the aid of my wealth.

Here, said Ingrid.

I stood up and she handed me a bouquet of flowers.

She said the flowers were for the lifesaver, not for the man with whom she had lived together and whom she once loved.

I've ordered coffee and beer, I answered.

She took a sip of the beer and made a face.

I told her an impious thought had occurred to me as I was rescuing the girl. While swimming I suddenly thought of the population explosion and wondered whether it wouldn't be best if I and the girl drowned.

She looked round as though searching for someone else in the cafe.

Who are you looking for?

She was just checking the place out, Ingrid answered; here was where we'd gotten to know each other. She said she would've preferred a different place to meet, but this Morler character could not be persuaded otherwise.

The waitress came by.

My wife would like champagne. Bring us a bottle!

Are you really going to run?

The afternoon was past. A boundless joy over my wealth took hold of me. Was I not rich enough to cast off forever the cage of guilt feelings in which I'd lived for so long?

Who told you about that? I asked in turn, myself becoming curious.

Oh please, she answered impatiently, as if I knew exactly who it was and was just trying to make her look foolish: Morler, for instance, who's been coming and going lately as if he were a friend of the family.

This Morler, I said, is a devious customer; you can't believe a word he says.

The waitress came with the bottle. Guests looked over at us, curious as to who was drinking champagne, champagne in broad daylight.

Oh, take it away, please, Ingrid admonished, when the waitress showed her the bottle, and the girl turned to me. I nodded, the bottle was opened.

Her anger had made my former wife more beautiful and I became tentative in my judgment that I had long considered final.

She said that Bergius had run the city well and she wanted him to continue to do so. But the love between them was no longer what it had been …

I pushed a glass towards her and, lost in thought as she was, she drank from it.

She said she was prepared to come back to me if I so wished and if I promised not to run against Bergius.

I had to end this madness before it was too late.

I told her she was operating on the assumption that I still loved her. That was the case up until four weeks ago, but no longer, I said. Since then I had become a totally different person and no longer desired her sacrifice. My idea now was to live for the moment, without ties, subject only to my own whims.

As I spoke these words, I began more and more to believe what I was saying.

That meant I could promise her ten times over not to run, but then do it anyway based on a whim.

I took her hand and stroked it.

Yes, I thought, maybe you *are* the harpy Gesellius thinks you are.

Don't cry, I said, although she was far from crying.

The waitress arrived at our table to refill, but actually out of curiosity.

Take the champagne away, I said, to get rid of her.

Is something wrong with it? Isn't it good?

No, no, I said, it's just that there's nothing to celebrate.

She shot a glance at me, looking me in the eye a tad longer than necessary, and I understood that I should come back, alone, and tell her all about it …

She took the half-full bottle and left.

If you're of a mind to start over without me, I said, and without the Latin teacher, if you should wish to leave here, say, go abroad, to New York, I would help you; I've come into some money.

I paid and left the cafe. The lights had been turned on. Outside it was getting dark and I saw Ingrid sitting at her place, head lowered, as if in thought or perhaps tears. And as I'm looking back, in my mind already back at the settlement, two passers-by almost jostle me off the narrow sidewalk, and I hear one of them say:

Yesterday at the Reithaus Restaurant, Morler sprang for bubbly.

38

Warm water covers me, but water is transparent, so I can see my body. Even when I was more handsome, in Krautmann's day, I was at odds with it. That's over. Now, finally, it belongs to me, like my name, my past, my wealth.

There's a racket going on downstairs, from Bausinger's apartment, as if someone has fallen down; for a moment it interrupts my thought process; then I am again thankful that there is a bathtub here in House One, in the attic, with hot running water at my disposal. Briefly I ruminate on the river and death, and that I must leave here and have no idea where to. And as I think about death, my glance falls upon the soap bowl, in which a very sharp knife lies open, a present from Krautmann, which I often place, open, next to the tub when bathing.

Here, a Finn knife, Krautmann had said, maybe at some point you'll find it useful. I give it to you because I like your book.

Whoever laughs or says kerchoo /
Will get his ass beat black and blue.

Tomorrow, or rather the day after, since I want to visit Armbruster tomorrow, I'll ask Morler about the Reithaus affair.

39

Time was when you could get rid of devils like me with money.

Gesellius says this with a smile and shakes his head a bit, unable to grasp that there's someone who can't be had for money.

I'd come into the city on the bus. The river was exuding mist; it was autumn. The bus crept through the gray wall with infinite sluggishness, and the few passengers huddled together, there being nothing but fog outside the windows.

What a fog, said the man sitting behind me. He was of my age, but less well dressed. He was sitting forward, his arms hanging over the seatback next to me, and I could see that he was wearing a watch on both left and right wrists. Two watches, I thought, one expensive, the other cheap.

These days he usually had to go into the city, he said, since there were no longer any stores in Backofen.

That might change, a woman said interrupting. Grissmann has promised to build a big supermarket with low-priced specials in the settlement. All we'd have to do is elect him mayor. Then Backofen would have the most beautiful supermarket, and the city folk would envy us and would have to come into the settlement to do quality shopping.

Who's this guy Grissmann? asked the man with the watches.

You don't know anything! the woman laughed at him.

We'd arrived and exited the bus.

Gesellius, I ask, aren't you going to offer me a coffee? For a coffee I'll give up my candidacy. Esau and the lentil pottage!

But Gesellius, formerly the wisecrack artist among Krautmann's assistants, cannot laugh about this and in memory of our former friendship I lay my hand on his knee and shake it in an effort to dispel his dark thoughts.

If only Krautmann were still here, he says. He had never wanted to be bank director.

I take my money and get up.

What's the deal with this candidacy of mine? Who's behind it? I ask on leaving. Is it Morler?

But Gesellius merely gives a bitter laugh.

The detention center is on the same street as the bank.

I climbed the steep street and broke a sweat. Suddenly the fog lifted. In front of me stood the prison gate.

Morler had taken care of the formalities and I only had to show my ID.

An officer led me into the meeting room, and when Armbruster appeared, the officer stayed with us. We sat at the table opposite each other, the judicial officer sitting at the head. Armbruster looked good, as if recuperated, a little like Einstein, only better groomed.

Grissmann, how nice to see you. But just what do you think you're doing?

Here, I said, handing him a box of sweets, Belgian chocolates.

He tore open the box and was about to sample it, then thought better of it and offered, first me, and then the officer, a treat.

Living alone, one becomes a solipsist and forgets one's manners. He laughed.

The officer declined, not permitted to eat on duty. I, however, indulged myself with a white truffle with dark filling.

Armbruster protested that I had no experience in directing or governing a city. What on earth had possessed me to stand for election to the mayoralty? Or was all that guff in the newspapers wrong?

The truffle melted in my mouth.

I asked him if the lawyer I'd procured for him had come by.

No, Armbruster answered hotly. My proxy agent, that Morler guy, had looked him up, that's all.

I looked into Armbruster's beautiful philosopher face; however, the noble mien he was now using so reproachfully annoyed me.

The officer was a man in late youth, bald and already sporting a paunch. As an athletic type he reminded me of my father, and I tried to imagine how it must feel to lie dead in the cemetery, under the earth, in his Grissmann grave.

He had a comment to make, the officer said, turning to Armbruster: He would vote for Grissmann. That lecherous, red-headed pecker had been in office too long. I, as a lifesaver, was a better man for the city.

We were silent. The two men looked at me, as though expecting something from me. I squinted into the sun's rays streaming through the window.

You should honor father and mother /
When they slap one cheek, don't turn the other /
When they around the corner spy /
You should punch them in the eye.

I am a free man, I said finally, and as such I possess the freedom not to decide.

But even as I said that, I was overwhelmed by an awareness of the endless possibilities arising from the abyss of decisions that opens up to every rich person. A vast cosmos of freedom enveloped me and threatened to devour me. I became dizzy and moved my seat out of the sun.

Armbruster, I said, needing to feel the ground under my feet again, isn't it a pity that, with our present understanding/ knowledge of religion, with the dying-out of any sort of Biblical knowledge, even the jokes about those subjects perish?

This means that man has no intuitive sense of far-distant things that play a part in our world. I looked out the window up to the moon. It was late, the thoughts of the day had fallen away from me, even the one that had accompanied me so insistently for quite some time now: that I am rich.

The light of the satellite was sacred—sobering like spring water, and in my mind I went on a trip. 384,000 kilometers. What was that anyway?

At one point I had the thought that I must speak with Morler tomorrow, at another, that I, known as I was, could not remain here in my familiar surroundings.

Then I shoved these thoughts aside and continued my journey …

40

Morler proposed that we hash it all out on a walk through the woods. The suggestion came from him; I merely agreed.

We'll take your path, your favorite path.

His voice on the phone sounded as if he were speaking with a child or a sick person.

We'd walked in silence for a while, and while the forest surrounded us, I found myself wishing to be alone on this walk. As we approached the forest, and the city lay beneath us, I wanted to say something, to give a hint at least that I might be leaving here and therefore would no longer be needing his services. However, it had struck me how fully he was enjoying nature just now. With transfigured face he gazed down over the fruited meadows upon city and stream.

You know that look, I thought. That's the way he looked in America when he took off across the field. I reached for his arm and held it fast.

What for, really? I thought. Why don't you let him loose to run into this marvelous landscape?

Smiling, with a gentle gesture, Morler removed my hand from his arm.

You don't have to run for office, Georg. You can go wherever you want; you're rich and free. But you could own this city.

With a grand gesture, he waved his arm down over the valley.

It's possible that my wealth and the fluctuations of fate in recent weeks had changed me—I slapped him.

We were both astonished by the force of the blow; his cheek turned red; the slap resounded. Morler stood there, at first startled, then sad. I wanted to observe his inward response.

As he now touched his cheek, the sleeve of his leather jacket rode up. On Morler's wrist was a tattoo, circling it like an armband. In blue, unadorned capital letters a name was legible: Helena.

I forgive you, Georg, Morler said and laughed. I have to forgive you, since it's by your grace that I live in the lap of luxury. He added that he needed new money to squander.

I took out the money Gesellius had given me and gave him most of it. I'll ask him about Helena later, I thought.

Are you going to treat everybody to champagne again at the Reithaus?

He didn't answer. For a while we gazed in silence into the autumnal valley. The sun, opposite us, gilded us as it began to go down.

Why won't you take Ingrid back, Morler said finally as he shivered; he'd grown cool.

Oh Morler, I answered, are you in love with her?

We shielded our eyes from the sun with our hands, and it occurred to me, since Armbruster was just now in jail, to talk to Morler about myself instead of him. The last rays of the sun lit up his burning cheek.

Morler, I said, you're the only one I can talk to about my wealth. In that instant it struck me that many of the old proverbs no longer applied to me, since I was rich. *Morning hour has gold in flower. Idleness is the devil's workshop. The child is father to the man.* That you have to grin and bear it with ambition, diligence, work and tenacity … It struck me that none of that concerned me any longer, and I didn't know if I was happy about that.

Morler gave me a sign to keep quiet. A mood of concord and peace had enveloped us, even though I had just struck him. He indicated I was not to destroy this aura, but rather to surrender myself to the sunset in silence.

We must have enjoyed the grand display for too long, for, as we entered the separating forest again, the darkness surprised us. I could barely see the path, yet when I strained my eyes, it seemed to me a bit brighter than the surrounding darkness. I went ahead, Morler following behind. The detective had taken out his cellphone. But as Morler tried to find the path by the light of his phone, we noted that the device was almost out of charge—the light went out.

In the darkness of the forest, I began to reproach Morler forcefully. I told him the reason I'd brought him here was to help me simplify my life—yet now with all this twaddle about my candidacy it had gotten more complicated. I said I hardly knew him anymore with all his exuberant *joie de vivre*. Just a few weeks earlier he'd been a melancholic …

We were standing still.

Quiet! said the detective softly.

And sure enough, from a distance we could hear, just barely, stomping music, punctuated by hooting and bawling.

That's the wurst stand! I know the way from there, said Morler, happy again and full of piss and vinegar. And as for my reproaches, I myself was to blame: If you had taken Ingrid's suggestion, you wouldn't have had to run for office.

Following the din, we stumbled our way along the overgrown paths to the bratwurst stand. The music and the hooting grew louder and louder.

Somebody had put up a beer tent in the clearing.

Hey, let's head for that!

Morler was as happy as a schoolboy that something was up.

As so often, when one wants to do something, but the other has reservations, I followed him. And a rule of Krautmann's occurred to me, one he had drilled into us: You must go there where you would rather not. Without the people you will not come to know your homeland.

A man stepped out of the brightly lit stand, someone I knew. It was the sad sack who had raised the blinds. He was carrying an enormous tray on which lay forty or fifty fried wurst, some burnt black, others pale, only slightly fried. Morler grabbed a wurst from the tray and immediately began eating it.

Then he held the entrance awning up for the wurst man. The three of us went into the tent together.

The place was bursting with people. They sat on benches at long tables, beer steins in front of them. At the front end opposite the entrance was a platform on which the band sat playing a Beatles song. A couple squeezed together and gave us a friendly nod. We'd scarcely sat down—the wurst man had moved on—when a young woman brought us beer. I wanted to pay but she shook her head: Everything was free. Our bench neighbors hoisted their steins for clinking.

What are you doing here? I thought, but the couple sitting next to me affected me with the joy they took in beer, wurst and music, and I raised my stein to them. From the corner of my eye, I could see that the detective also raised his.

The band ended their piece and all you could hear was the hum produced by a crowd of people in celebration. Then a man stepped to the microphone. It was Gesellius.

Once again, he said, he wanted to extend a warm welcome to one and all. How beautiful the mix of people was, many here from the city and many from Wennfelder Garten …

Morler nudged me, and as I turned to him, he pointed straight ahead towards the speaker with his stein and smirked.

The latter was expressing the sentiment that, if we were feeling good here, with the music, and the beer and the wurst, then we should give expression to that by rapping our steins on the table and applauding!

He paused; the tent turned silent; from outside you could hear the autumn wind in the trees; they moaned.

Then suddenly someone rapped with his beer stein; someone cried bravo, whooped the way musicians do in the Alps, a high-pitched, over-the-top "whoopee!" It was Morler.

Then the rapping engulfed the whole tent; even I myself rapped and shouted.

In a moment, I thought, as though I knew the future, in a moment Bergius will appear.

To one man, however, Gesellius cried into the mic, to one man do we especially give thanks for the fact that we sit here together in celebration today … Someone who has done so much for our city, who has advanced it … here he is, our host, the mayor!

Morler, I asked, did you know about this production?

He shook his head and I believed him.

Morler, I'd be a much worse mayor than he is!

The mayor began to talk about his time in office—though arraying the list of his accomplishments in the form of a confession: And then, he said in conclusion, almost in jest, he had committed one further sin. The new bus lines between the city and Wennfelder Garten —he almost said Backofen!

A long time ago, Krautmann had given a lecture on this kind of speech. Just then the title popped into my head: “Popular Speakers and Their Psychology.” The gist of it, of course, was that this kind of orator was doomed to extinction, along with his audience.

There was a huge wave of laughter and applause. My bench neighbor turned towards me and nodded in agreement.

My people, I have sinned, I have confessed. I would like to continue to be your mayor. Will you keep an old sinner like me?

Gesellius has rehearsed this with him, I thought. No doubt Gesellius helped him write the speech.

Bergius gestured and a woman in the first row stood up and went up onto the stage. She took up a position next to her husband, took his hand and smiled to the audience.

Even though I had rejected her offer, my heart contracted to see her standing up there, next to her unfaithful husband, looking so beautiful.

Let’s go, Morler!

Just five more minutes, the detective asked.

I’ll be leaving this city, I said. Then I won’t be needing your services any longer.

It was as if I had merely thought that, not spoken it. Morler didn’t react, merely staring fixedly at the stage.

He’s about to make a mistake, Morler said.

One more thing, Bergius said: Along with him they would also be electing his charming wife, whose concern for the welfare of the city is known to all.

At that point he wanted to leave. Gesellius stood ready to speak the closing remarks and end the festival. The band members raised their instruments.

For a moment one heard the moaning and groaning of the trees.

Then the mayor stepped up to the microphone again.

There was, he said, someone who wanted to run against him. But even though this man had rescued a child, no one knew anything else about him: Although he lived in Wennfelder Garten, this man was very rich.

He pointed at me.

You're rich and free, I thought. If you like, you can leave now; if not, you can stay and see what happens.

Morler walked to the front, jumped up on stage and took the microphone.

A rich man is not so easily corrupted!

He signaled the band and it made a flourish.

Now we can go, the detective said.

I stood up, bowed my head and left the tent.

The wind had picked up, the trees sighed and moaned. The moon hung over the clearing; clouds covered it up only to set it free again.

41

I'm living with my mother now. She doesn't hold it against me that I'm rich. The only thing that miffed her was that she had to learn this fact from the newspaper. These days I often listen to her practice the texts she has to recite during her tours. She's always forgetting them. From listening I'm learning a great deal about my family. My father never talked about anything else, but I wasn't interested then. I'm also making myself useful in the housekeeping. I've got the family history in my left hand, the vacuum cleaner in my right. I go around the apartment like this, my mother following me as she recites her text, very loud, to drown out the machine. She has to speak up for the tourists, so it's a good exercise for her.

Do you really want to be mayor?

I don't know, I tell her, and continue: Who was rector of the university in the eighteenth century and what was his significance? The answer is that this Rector Grissmann denied the Copernican teaching.

Election posters are being put up for you everywhere! Who's doing this, against your will?

Morler, I answer, probably my employee Morler.

Would you be proud if I were mayor?

She said she'd had hopes I would become a professor.

And we continue with the family history, until she interrupts herself again.

There's a fellow in the riding club restaurant who's springing for champagne almost every day. It was in the paper. Is that this Morler character?

During the day now, I sit a lot in the children's room and think about myself. Evenings I play Solitaire in the living room and drink beer. Thus do the days pass, and the election, which I mostly don't think about, draws near. At our last meeting I ordered Morler to announce that I was not a candidate, but he didn't do it—on the contrary, he's holding rallies in my name. Most recently, I've stopped reading the newspaper and I've even forbidden my mother to read to me from it. I don't want to know anything about the surveys in which I'm up one day and down the next in the voters' favor.

When I go out into the city, I don't like it, and so I avoid it as far as possible. But many routes are unavoidable. Today I have to see Gesellius for fresh funds.

I'll be visiting father's grave on the way back, I say at breakfast. I ask what kind of flowers I should buy for the occasion.

And as I watch her sitting there, even at breakfast bent over her texts, I make a mental note to give her flowers too. You don't have to do this job, I tell her, adding that I can give her as much money as she wants.

She thanks me for the offer, but I sense her disapproval.

Yesterday evening, I tell her, when you were in bed and I still in the living room, I was once again very happy.

Sometimes on the street I would imagine I were a tabula rasa, a stranger walking through a beautifully restored old downtown, able to go anywhere I liked, north or south, out beyond the city or up castle hill. Then I would see a poster on a wall. And although the man in the picture could just as easily have been Morler, still it was my name printed on the bottom, so I wasn't a stranger at all, but an agitator.

I was on my way to the bank. Passersby eyed me in the pedestrian zone, unsure, and several greeted me, just in case. I returned their greetings, reluctantly at first, then with a smile, finally with a small hand gesture, campaigner through and through.

How many fewer posters than Morler did the strongman-cum-Latin-teacher hang!

At the entrance to the bank, I stopped to test my voice. I was calm and in good humor, without those spikes of euphoria that so often cause anxiety.

Gesellius, I called out, even before his office door had closed behind us. Gesellius, you have betrayed our secret! But even though you are bank director here, for sure there is someone in the far-off central bank who stands over you. To him I will bring your breach of trust to light!

It was my aim to scare Gesellius; it was just a joke. By now it was a matter of indifference to me whether people knew about my wealth. But the old blithe spirit showed no alarm. His face was pallid, with a strange air of contraction, such that I was gripped by pity and was already regretting my threat.

Please, Georg, Gesellius answered, I haven't betrayed anything. It was your friend Morler who told the mayor.

What's the matter? I asked. You look terrible. He was always the handsomest among Krautmann's assistants.

Is something bothering you? Are you ill?

He didn't answer but walked over to the little safe that stood unobtrusively in a corner of the office, removed a stack of banknotes and placed them in front of me. His movements were slow, as if he had to struggle to remember them.

Here.

Is it because I threatened you? But that would have no point, I told him, if he wasn't the one who informed the mayor.

I was an agitator, someone who had brought strife to the city and meant to cast aside a worthy man, the bank director answered in a soft voice. Of course, this was no surprise to him. Once a long time ago, Krautmann had singled me out for comment and, his tongue loosened by wine, the professor was moved to make assertions one normally doesn't make in the presence of colleagues and friends of the person under discussion. But it wasn't only that. It was something of incomparably deeper gravity.

His secretary brought in coffee, and Gesellius got right to it, already topping up his cup before I'd even taken my first sip.

He was plagued by doubts about the meaning of life, he said, in a somewhat firmer voice. Metaphysical consolation wasn't accessible to him, and he had no one to talk to about these doubts; his wife, and even Bergius, laughed at him when he approached them on the subject. There were many days, he said, when he would believe them; on others, like today, he wouldn't. On days like this, he couldn't stand himself, and, to avoid thinking about himself, he would place his persona entirely in the service of others, so that it would, in effect, dissolve ... Today, however, that was not working.

He was blushing and was ashamed. And yet he looked a bit fresher than before.

From earlier times I recalled such situations, and similar strategies for combatting them. I know what you mean, I said, then adding, however, that, for me as a rich man now, the issue was moot.

He went on to speak of the envy he secretly nourished towards already dead schoolmates; I agreed with him.

42

Today, for the first time—with my mother feeling ill this morning—I led a group of tourists through the Grissmann House. I have a good memory; from constantly listening to my mother, I knew the texts by heart.

All participants must put on felt slippers over their street shoes to spare the valuable floors. After collecting the entrance fees, I asked whether they all understood German, and they nodded. Behind the cash box there hangs a family tree, and, in response to the question of an older man as to whether the tours were, in fact, given by family members and where, in particular, I stood on the family tree, I answered that I was not yet inscribed but that my father was. One woman called out that there was no more room on the scroll for me. To prevent the tourists from suspecting fraud on my part, I took out my ID card and let it circulate.

Grissmanns with the forename Georg were rare, I said; only one of my forebears had my name, a scholar and rector of the university in the 18th century, a man who denied the Copernican system.

They laughed as if it were a joke.

It seemed to me as though I'd always been giving this tour. After the first room, my voice became powerful, animated, and I noticed how my interest in the family history, at first feigned but then genuine, began to intrigue my listeners. The illustrious episodes I described in a proud, upbeat tome; the demise, the eventual forced sale of the house, with halting voice and lowered head.

I must have done well, since, when I showed the tourists out at the end of the tour, they thanked me, and everyone gave me a big tip—as though wishing to console me over the decline of my family.

The next tour wasn't until that afternoon, so I went over to our apartment, made an herbal tea and brought it to my mother's bedside.

Here, I said, the tips.

I laid the money on the bedcover.

So much! my mother exclaimed. That's more than I ever got.

Beginner's luck, I replied. That's the kind of money your father made for decades, I thought.

That afternoon I had two more groups. I could test myself as to whether this kind of activity might already be starting to bore me. No: Since I was now more experienced, I found opportunities to look around some of the rooms, and the genealogy, told to me a hundred or a thousand times by my father, now arrayed itself before me like a grand historical tapestry, a tapestry that allowed me to forget my current life for a while.

My mother got up for dinner; she was feeling a little better. From our living room you could see the Grissmann House on the other side of the street, and

I pointed over there in order to bring the beauty of the illuminated facade to my mother's attention.

I hadn't thought of Morler once that day. Now, as the doorbell rang, he came to mind.

Who's ringing so late? I huffed.

After dinner my mother should go to bed early, I figured, while I, after a successful day, was looking forward to another beer while relaxing in the living room.

My mother went to get the door. I could tell by her voice it was someone she didn't know. I couldn't understand what she was saying, nor his words either, but I did hear him laugh. My mother hesitated to let him in, and in reaction to that his laughter grew louder.

I felt as though I knew this situation: You believe you're merely a witness; it's only by accident that you overhear anything. Then, however, everything changes.

What's this business about you giving away champagne at the riding club?

It's for your son, Morler answered.

They came into the living room, my mother's face hidden by a huge bunch of gladiolas, behind her Morler, a bottle of champagne in his hand.

I could see it bothered him to see me sitting there at the dinner table in the living room, a plate of buttered bread and cheese before me, a glass of beer nearby. He turned away, toward the window, through which the facade of the Grissmann House shined.

Do you need new money, Morler?

I had the money on me; all I had to do was reach into my pocket, pull it out, divide the banknotes into two unequal halves and give him the larger one. Without regard to my mother, he stuck it in his pocket.

Without Morler I wouldn't be rich, I said.

She set another place for dinner. I went into the kitchen to get our guest a beer, and after taking the bottle from the fridge, I hesitated returning to the living room. Right now you could leave the apartment undetected, I thought, and by the time they noticed your absence, you'd be long gone.

Softly I padded into the hallway. If you raised the apartment door a bit, it made no noise clicking shut.

There I stood on the street, rich and free. Who didn't dream of this? A grand exultation seized me. The old city was empty of people and quiet; my footsteps in my new shoes echoed between the apartment building and the Grissmann House. Their echo would bring my mother to the window immediately and I would be exposed—I paused to consider what bound me to this place more: my mother's apartment or the Grissmann House.

No one had noticed my escape attempt. When I came back into the living room, my mother and Morler were sitting on the sofa drinking champagne and discussing my chances in the election.

So I've fetched this beer for nothing, I said.

Something was out of order: It wasn't our usual champagne glasses the two of them were drinking from, rather they were old hand-cut goblets. My mother must have pilfered them from the museum.

The voters, Morler said, continuing his bloviating, the voters love diversion. Pericles himself would've been recalled, had he not died of plague before the fact.

The champagne had done my mother good; the sickly woman of this morning had disappeared, her face all cheerful and young.

I had left my homeland a loser, Morler said, and was now returning as a rich man—what story could the mayor offer to counter that? The fact that only he, and not the candidate himself, was showing up for the various events was only titillating the curiosity of the masses even further.

And if he has no interest in becoming mayor? the woman on the sofa cried out.

Mother, where did you get those glasses?

Borrowed, and not even that. Basically they belong to us!

There were only two goblets at hand, so I drank beer.

He had something to confess to her, Morler said. In the beginning, he had only wanted to have some fun here in the city. But then he fall in love with the mayor's wife. She, however, wanted nothing to do with him; and so he would have his revenge.

Let's just not have the two of you falling in love with each other! I joked. A moment ago, on the street,

I was feeling strong and free, and enjoying being alone. Now I was back in society.

Morler raised his finger as though having forgotten something; then he retrieved from the vest pocket of his jacket some sort of notebook or booklet. He'd had to squeeze it together, otherwise it would've been too big for his pocket.

Here, said Morler, looking at my mother, his little book. I'd like him to autograph it.

Oh, that, she answered.

Listen up, Morler urged, and recited: "*On the isle of America, gorgeous girls abound hurrah …*" He said he found that highly interesting, reminding him as it did of his youth. Sign it, Georg! He handed me a fountain pen.

I set about the dedication. "For Morler from Georg"; I could think of nothing else. But the golden pen scratched along the bad paper and no ink came out of it.

Morler, I will not stand for election. You should leave the area and forget your love.

The two of us considered this in silence.

I'm going to bed, I said finally; I'll handle the first tour tomorrow.

Don't forget, Morler called after me, your big day is coming soon!

From bed I could hear the sound of their glasses, Morler's loud voice, the softer voice of my mother and their mingled laughter. Tomorrow I would put the goblets back in their display cases.

Later I awoke briefly. It was quiet. The lighting of the Grissmann house facade had gone out.

You have resolved to live for the sake of your moods and whims, I said to myself. I felt almost viscerally the pressure coming at me from that huge, dark structure.

43

I believe I've become rich at the right moment in my life. If the thing had happened earlier, it would've thrown me off track, and I would've wasted and squandered my fortune, on luxuries or high-flown projects. Later, on the other hand, I would've been an older man, exposed at every turn to the anxiety of reading something in the financial news that would cause my dream of security and independence to collapse. I have cast off the optimism of youth, and my old hope of those days of becoming rich and independent at some point through achievement or luck, I had long since given up. When I look back on the event—is it really just a few weeks ago?—, I feel that God or some other planner of human destinies could not have chosen a better point in time. You see, I no longer consider money to be of any great consequence. Maturity! Strange word in this context. I'll have to ask Armbruster about it next time I visit him.

I found the goblets in the kitchen, washed and dried, walked over to the window and held them up to the light: not a crack, not a chip to be seen. I washed them a second time and dried them carefully. From my mother's bedroom, I could hear her snoring through the thin walls. Hadn't my father's snoring always been a problem for her in the past?

I put the glasses in a bag before taking them out into the street.

When I restored them to their showcase in the Grissmann House, they clinked against other valuable glasses, and a fine, expensive tingling resonated, and I recalled the pronouncement Morler had made to me yesterday: Your big day is coming soon!

I couldn't get that sentence out of my head and began to mull it over: Had there ever been big days in my life, and, if so, which days were they; during the first tour, a school class of nine-year-old pupils, I became certain I had never had a big day.

Please stop droning on like that!

They'd told her an older woman would be her tour guide, the teacher said; she had no idea who I was.

Georg Grissmann, the son, I answered, as I showed her my ID. They all wanted to see it, so she let it circulate. His grandparents and his great-grandparents and *their* parents had lived in this magnificent house in earlier times, hundreds of years ago, she told them. The children looked at me with admiration.

I took pains, and the kids listened to me attentively. In the next-to-last room, however, where the tour gets around to the text concerning the shoemaker, the downfall and the selling of the palace, there arose among the children, even before I had mentioned the shoemaker, a murmur. I wanted to wait until they had settled down, but then out of the murmur I distinguished a word, and now they cried out loud and pointed at me: mayor, mayor!

Oh, it's you, said the teacher. She said she had attended my campaign events and was astonished at how lopsidedly, how hatefully, my representative had ranted against the rich—that was too much for her. Still, she would vote for me.

She smiled at me.

Morler! I thought, what the hell are you doing, what skullduggery have you been up to!

I returned her smile.

When they were gone, I retrieved the goblets from the showcase and took them home with me.

44

One more time I will look up all the people who have been of significance to me here in the city. Krautmann will not be among them, a painful lacuna in my life.

I told my mother I wanted to go to my father's grave. I said that, since I now knew from my own experience how he spent his life, I was drawn back to that spot again. Could she please take over the next tour for me?

It was a mild Fall day, cemetery weather, I thought. I bought flowers at the cemetery entrance, laid them on my father's grave and thought about him. I didn't feel sadness. But it did occur to me that he had loved me well and that moved me. Then, from the poet's grave at which I'd recently seen Morler and the mayor together, I heard someone weeping—the weeping of a man.

I couldn't see him right off, he was almost entirely concealed by the poet's gravestone, and it wasn't until I moved closer that I recognized him. It was Bergius.

I was just at my father's grave, I said. He wiped away his tears.

Are you going to defeat me?

It was out of my hands, I answered.

Bergius laughed saying he'd come here to reflect. He said he did that often, coming to the poet's grave and reflecting.

The sun had come out and was highlighting his red hair.

He said he often felt compelled to think of a verse, a line of the poet's, and would at such times be overwhelmed by the beauty of the language. He never wept over politics, he claimed, but was helpless under the sway of this poetry.

Poems that had captivated me in this way came immediately to mind. *"Let man try everything … and grasp the freedom to sally forth wherever he will,"* I quoted. How beautifully that mirrored my current situation!

That was one of his favorite passages! the mayor exclaimed. He longed for school, for teaching, Bergius continued, suddenly waxing impetuous. But he didn't want to go back there as a loser.

Bergius, I tried to assuage him, you were a good Latin teacher. Even if at times a sadist. As for the rest, I told him I didn't think I had a chance against him.

Do you really think so? Bergius mewled. Then call off that bloodhound of yours, Morler!

Morler has his own mind, I said, and besides I was in his debt since he'd made me rich.

He left and I was alone in the cemetery. And while I remained standing between the grave of the poet and the gravestones of my family, it occurred to me that my original intention in summoning Morler had been to make my life simpler.

Copernicus, you swine! I thought, as I again passed by the grave of my ancestor, the denier. How insignificant you've made us all!

Whom should I look up today? I wondered the next day. Gesellius with his constant tirades, with his *idée fixe* that I'm an agitator?

In the pedestrian zone, people passing by smiled at me. Go ahead, smile, I thought, throw me stolen glances! I'll do whatever the hell I please!

In the minutes before arriving at the bank, I made a mental comparison of moments in which I'd been free and tried to rank them by the degree of freedom. It seemed to me I had never in my life been freer than on the ride through America.

A girl was coming out of the bank as I was going in, and we bumped into each other.

She was back from the big city, she said, before I could ask. It was nice to run into me, and she'd seen the posters.

Ah, the posters! I laughed and invited her for a coffee. Withdrawing money could wait. She too a homecomer, I thought.

It was all over with the mayor, she said. They'd parted without animosity.

I listened with half an ear; it felt good to be in her company.

What's that, I asked, what's that?

She repeated her question: Did I want to become mayor?

I said I'd much rather take her to see my mother and take over the tours of the Grissmann House. I wasn't sure, I answered.

Britta said I looked so melancholy. You can't become mayor that way.

When one is melancholy, one must take one's leave, I answered.

She had no apartment, said the girl. In case I wanted to visit her, she was staying at the Krone. That was Morler's doing. It was my money, not his, he'd assured me.

I nodded and went off to the bank, she in the opposite direction.

45

Soon the afternoon would be here to weaken me. I didn't want to face Gesellius in a weakened condition. You'll collect money from him only one more time, after that never again if possible.

Shortly before twelve I entered Gesellius' office.

Gesellius, I need more money than usual, I greeted him.

He didn't answer, didn't even look up, but rather stared fixedly at the monitor that hung across from his desk. Ordinarily, I now recalled, it showed stock-price quotations or programs on the stock exchange or the economy, sound muted. I was curious as to what had him so fascinated and stepped up next to him. Someone was singing and dancing there, even though you heard nothing; then they would cut back to a rapturous audience. It was a child who was moving like an adult, a boy about six years old. And then, as Gesellius switched from mute to sound, you could hear him singing too. He sang loud and coarse, just like his paragon, only higher. But the dance movements, rebellious and manly when done by his idol, had a titillating and obscene effect coming from a child. The singer was wearing his white Elvis costume.

"You ain't nothin' but a hound dog …"

Gesellius hummed along softly with the music, even swinging his hips a bit while sitting. Remember?

Krautmann? Krautmann was a big fan of Elvis, I said. During Fasching Krautmann always wore that white, spangled costume.

The singer had finished and the camera panned the audience, settling on a woman who was applauding enthusiastically: Helena.

But that's not what he wanted to show me, he said. He changed channels, and volumes of numbers raced across the screen. Do you know what this means? He laughed an unhappy laugh. It meant that his small fortune and the very large one that had fallen into my lap could soon be totally gone.

Then give me more money, twice as much as usual!

I sounded reckless. And yet a dread was coming over me that, at a moment's notice, my life could change radically for the second time.

The afternoon announced itself. It was just this outrageous sentence that I still managed to cough up. I took the pile of cash that Gesellius had counted out for me and stormed out of there without a word to anyone.

Two days from now would be Sunday. Election Sunday.

My mother was thrilled by my suggestion to take her out to the Reithaus; in recent years my father had taken her out only very seldom; and as early as five, as I lay on the bed in the children's room feeling the afternoon as it wound down, she had begun her preparations for the evening.

When I came back from the evening tour—the patrons were residents of an old people's home—I was met by a meticulously made-up, elegant woman, even if a bit too youthfully dressed for her age.

She said she was having doubts whether she should go with me, fearing that people might regard her outfit as too young. Might it not be better if I went alone and told her all about it afterward; might not a report about it, in fact, be better than the reality itself?

Come with me, I replied. Who knows where I'll be tomorrow or the day after! At least for one more time we will have done something together. And here, I said, I've brought this bonnet for you from the museum.

I brought the bonnet out from behind my back and carefully placed it on her head.

She looked at herself in the mirror and said nothing. The bonnet looked very good on her. My mother looked in the mirror and cried. How lucky, I thought, that it's your mother and not some other woman with whom you couldn't tell what she was thinking or feeling, or how you might win her.

The taxi for which I'd called arrived shortly before nine. It was the same cabby who had once driven me to the Backofen Settlement, the one who was mugged in the separating forest.

I told him we had to wait a moment as I climbed into the back seat of the cab, that my mother hadn't yet decided if she wanted to come along. He could just let the meter run. I asked him whether he'd ever picked up this Morler character.

Oh sure, in fact he'd just picked him up from the Krone and let him out in front of the Reithaus. Just as on many other evenings, unless a colleague snapped the fare away from him. The only way Morler ever went anywhere was in a taxi.

Listen, I finally interrupted him, I'm rich and I hate delays. To the Reithaus! Step on it!

Hey, I know you! the cabby suddenly exclaimed as he eyed me in the rearview. And it was this brief utterance, this tiny delay, that allowed my mother, who had appeared in the door window as a silhouette, to climb in just in time.

At the Reithaus

46

The Reithaus Hotel stood on a plateau slightly above the city. The Equestrian Sports Club had purchased property and built there: a riding arena, stables, a clubhouse-cum-restaurant, originally only for members. To this day an air of exclusivity has pervaded the restaurant "Zum Reithaus."

I myself had never been there and only knew of the place from an incident that had occurred there: Shortly after its opening, Krautmann had run amok in the Reithaus. He'd been drunk, so he told us the next day in the coolest of tones, without the least regret or braggadocio. He really busted the place up.

Guests crowded together in front of the entrance. From behind, newcomers impatiently shoved their way past us. I asked my mother if I shouldn't doff my incognito, which would allow us to simply bypass the line. But she was enjoying being among people; the closeness, the jostling, perhaps even the gazes of men coming her way delighted her.

From where we were standing, we could see through the open door into the interior of the place. It was a large, prosaic room, the tables and chairs in Scandinavian style. Pictures of horses hung on the walls. All tables were occupied.

So this is where Krautmann ran amok. I now regretted taking my mother here. What would she think if I now proceeded to bust everything up here?

A big man in a dark suit was blocking the way in.

Did I have reservations? the man asked politely.

Who are you? St. Peter? I shouted, loud enough to be heard by those behind us. The laughter grew loud. I turned to my mother behind me. As nice as the youthful dress had just looked on her, she now seemed lost in it. A great disappointment lay on her face.

All you need do is tell them who you are, I thought.

From the depths of the room a man came out to us, spread his arms out and smiled.

Hold on, Matthias, he said to the man in the dark suit. This is Grissmann, Georg Grissmann.

Matthias apologized to me, saying he hadn't recognized me right off.

Morler took my mother by the hand and led her into the room. I followed them.

As we passed by the tables, the guests looked up, many applauding or waving to us.

You should be better known, said Morler, as we sat down at his table. But don't worry about it!

I greeted the other guests at our table, there being maybe ten. I didn't know any of them—correction: Way down at the other end sat Ingrid, my ex.

Nice of you to drop by for a change, Morler said, not waiting for my reaction, however, but turning again to my mother, who sat on his other side. I took a look around.

Are you the new mayor? asked my neighbor, turning to me. It was one of the students who had enjoyed the free champagne here; the wild hairstyle and the piercing eyes revealed rather the fanatic than the freeloader.

I would certainly have his vote, assuming, that is, the great destroyer for whom everyone was basically waiting did not show up at the last second.

Him I could tell, it occurred to me, that I was toying with the idea of busting up the joint here.

Are you bored, Georg? asked Morler. I can tell just by looking at you. That's the problem with you rich types!

And in fact I *had* begun to feel bored. And you? I asked. Isn't boredom also the reason you're doing all of this?

Morler was evasive, saying he always liked to have a live band on tap. When he thought the mood was just right, he'd give the signal, they'd play and people could dance.

With that a silence enveloped the table for a moment, that being the only reason I could hear what Ingrid spoke into this silence: I only came here to dance.

A profound equanimity came over me. You can put an end to all of this nonsense, I thought. All you need do is not give Morler any more money.

When Ingrid said that, Morler, looking lovestruck and miserable, got up and raised his hand. That was the signal, and four musicians came in and climbed the platform in a corner of the room.

My mother asked Morler if he'd like to dance with her, and Morler reacted as if he'd been waiting for just that.

I didn't particularly want to watch this unlikely couple dance, both of whom had had such a great influence on my life, and gazed in a different direction.

Do you want to dance with me? Ingrid said, coming up to me. If not, I'll dance alone. Ah, could we wait a bit, this is not my number.

She sat down on Morler's seat and, perhaps out of inattentiveness, drank from Morler's glass.

Bergius has disappeared, Ingrid said. She hadn't seen him since yesterday. It feels just like that time with Krautmann. Even on the day before his disappearance, he struck us as changed, as though transparent, not quite fully there.

Yes. We noticed it and couldn't do a thing about it. Back then Krautmann had no good reason, Ingrid continued. Now with Bergius it's different: Morler and I had really driven him from the city.

I took her hand and led her onto the dance floor, the way Morler had just done with my mother.

The tune the band was now playing was old. It was a tune to which I, as a schoolboy, had practiced dancing in front of the mirror. Now my body recalled it all, the moves coming of themselves. Ingrid had always been a good dancer.

The music ended. From somewhere I thought I heard the sounds of wrath and the crashing of overturned tables, but I could find nothing in the room to explain the racket. Then the music began to play again.

Where would I have preferred to be just then? In my attic, maybe.

Here, said a voice behind me, what should I do with him?

I turned around. Bergius was standing there. In front of him he held, in a hammerlock, the student who had sat next to me. The student twisted and turned, fighting against the hold, but Bergius held him effortlessly.

He said he wanted to hand the hooligan over to Morler.

Morler would be right here, I said, he's dancing with my mother.

Bergius looked at me with amusement, as if I were leaving everything to Morler, impotent to do anything on my own. I took the hooligan from him and was now holding him in a hammerlock myself. On our way to the exit, as we passed the broken chairs, the student again tried to free himself. But even *I* was too strong for him.

Here, Matthias, a hooligan, throw him out.

It occurred to me that maybe I should ask Bergius to let me come with him, in case he left the city. I waited till the band took a break, placed my hands before my mouth like a megaphone and shouted to the room:

Bergius, you red-headed woodpecker! Take me with you when you leave the city!

Everybody turned towards me and laughed.

He was long gone.

Morler had come up to me:

If it becomes known tomorrow that he's leaving the city, you'll be mayor the day after.

He wants to teach Latin again. And me, Morler? What do I want?

Morler, however, was off to the other end of the table to have a word with Ingrid. It was clear that he was professing his love to her and that she was refusing him.

47

I'm sitting in the Blue Room, in the Rococo Room. Winter sun is shining in through the window, falling on the secretary made of bright wood, falling on the ornate inlaid work on the doors of the cabinet above the writing surface: earth, sun, moon and stars. It was on just such a secretary in the year of the French Revolution that Georg Grissmann penned his screed against Copernicus, and thus the inlaid work shows the heavens as my ancestor wished them to be. We are the center, we ourselves!

I've been here for three days now, and the fancy chair of the denier has become my favorite spot. Here I sit reflecting on my life, while in front of me the earth rules the sun. But whenever I try to feel my way into a world in which we are at the center—the feeling of importance fails to arise in me.

For the moment I most prefer the Blue Room, and I have my meals served here, even though it's impractical, the kitchen being in the basement and the room on the second floor. The dishes easily grow cold.

I tell Edna how easy it is to hear her footsteps when she brings my food in this quiet house, how long it takes for her to reach the Blue Room from the landing below! You could measure the spaciousness of the building by this, a fact that now, for the first time, fills me with pride of ownership.

She smiled her friendly smile, and I noticed that she was glad I was back and now had something to do and a person to talk to—she had taken care of my house all alone during my absence.

I have no idea what she thinks of me. Sometimes I see her outside standing at the grave of my predecessor, her head bowed. Maybe he became a bad fellow later on. Before that, though, Edna tells me in answer to my question, he performed good works with his wealth. But after a while, he seemed to lose every impulse to do that.

Edna is a believer, pious even, and when she talks about his good works, she smiles with rapture.

I'm never bored for a second here! I only miss Armbruster a little and, now and then, a girl like Britta. All the rest, I think, sitting on the copy of the denier's chair, which I've moved to the window, all the others over there can take a flying leap! and I gaze out into the winter garden, which the sun, our mistress and sovereign, mildly illuminates. I should take Armbruster in when he's released, and maybe my mother too. But she has to attend to the museum. No one else but her, for whom the Grissmann House meant so little that my father accused her of not loving him, and she had to assure him that she did love him, but only as an individual. The walls of our apartment are thin, and whenever I would hear these conversations from the children's room, I would hold my ears closed.

Outside the bullfinch is singing, and through the Blue Room window I see him in his blazing blue; and now that I can see and hear him again, it occurs to me that I once scooted over to my parents' bedroom and cried out: Don't talk about it! Stop! Stop!

For this evening I've invited Edna to keep me company at dinner; she should cook something she herself would like to eat. She suggested an old Slavic dish from the south, roast pork with red beans. While he could still eat, Wilhelm enjoyed this dish, even inviting her once to share it with him.

Edna, I finally called out to her, I know you like to drink red wine. Bring up a nice bottle for this evening.

To the Blue Room, Georg?

We ate early since I like to go to bed early. The meal was spicy and delicious, and I praised Edna for it. This dish was for holidays only, she said, usually it was just beans and rice.

We spoke little, almost nothing, but neither of us was embarrassed by that, and I watched the way she drank the wine, with half-closed eyes.

I asked her if it wasn't one of the best wines in the cellar?

Oh no, she answered indulgently, as if to a foolish question. Herr Grissmann had wines of a quite superior caliber down there! Then she asked if she might put a question to me.

As long as it wasn't too personal, I answered.

She liked to watch TV. Her departed husband's favorite program and now, in his memory, hers too: "Strange Happenings from around the World." Europe was often on the show, and in a small city there was a race for mayor. The name of the city struck her as familiar. Possibly Herr Grissmann had mentioned it.

Really? I asked, without intending it as a question.

And they showed pictures, she said, of the mayor and the challenger. It was an older man running against a younger one.

Nothing unusual about that, I said.

Edna made a gesture indicating I should not interrupt her.

On election Sunday, it turned out that both candidates had left the city; nobody knew for where.

She had leaned forward and was looking me in the face. Nonsense, I thought, she doesn't suspect a thing; she's just high on the good wine.

But there was a third man there, she continued.

She got up to get the dessert, and when she came back I thought that she might have forgotten the whole business in the interval.

And this third man, Edna went on, was Morler, the man who brought me here last time.

And? I said. What happened then?

The younger man won. Now the city council is debating whether his representative should not be permitted to take over the office on an interim basis …

You would've become a good mayor. Or was that not you, the younger one, the election winner?
No, I said, that wasn't me.

Her face released its tension. This issue might easily have cast a pall over our entire evening.

She left to make coffee, and, while she was gone, it occurred to me that she and Armbruster would've gotten along famously.

Here, she said, when she came back. My predecessor had often smoked a cigar with his coffee, while he was allowed to and was up to it. She loved to smell the smoke. Wouldn't I like to light one up myself?

Sure, I thought, why not? Then I thought of the bullfinch and how little we know of life.

Last night, I said, I dreamed that I was rich.

Once in a while, she had that dream too, Edna replied. We laughed over the world's peculiarity.

Today, against my will, three men pulled up here.

I was in the park, pondering the question whether it was possible to declare a certain place to be one's home, then, maybe, after a given period of time, to withdraw the same support, these same energies, from this self-made home just as from a traditional, inherited one.

I was in the park when I heard the crunch of tires against the gravel path in the distance. The noise came closer, sharp and bright in the winter air. It was morning; I wasn't afraid. Two limousines pulled up. Both were driven by chauffeurs in uniform, who, however, remained in the vehicles and couldn't be clearly seen through the windshield.

Hello, George.

The lawyer. The notary from New York, whom I knew from my first stay here.

Out of the second car climbed two young men in dark suits who now joined us.

Mormons, I thought. They look like twins. Mormon twins. What are they doing here?

Greg, of course, Greg! Capable men these two, said Greg, and they were deeply involved in the management of my empire.

Aren't they Mormons, I asked in German, who want to hide me away someplace where I'd spend the rest of my days in supreme bliss?

Edna met us in the hallway: She said she had told the caller yesterday that I didn't want any visitors; she thought they would respect that.

Never mind! I interjected. Bring us coffee in the denier's room—she, however, looked nonplussed—in the Blue Room.

Everything was going well, Greg said, his large athletic frame hardly suited to the dainty chair, and even the Mormons and I myself sat in the Blue Room as if on kiddy furniture, furniture for dwarves. Greg said he had wanted to see me in person and to introduce Tom and Harry to their employer.

The two of them smiled at me, extending their hands, which I took and shook. The pressure of their hands was at once strong and calming, like the pressure of angel hands. Yes, this comparison also explained their beauty, which had an oddly sterile effect, and their youth, which, though I put it at about the mid-twenties, yet had something about it that was independent of time.

I'm a worm next to them, I thought, and yet they work for me.

Tom and Harry had a nickname in the company—may I mention it, Greg asked, and both nodded—the archangels.

They had spreadsheets with them and other documents which they showed me; I glanced at these, and when Greg again reminded me how well things were going for the company, my company, I praised them and was amazed at the pleasure my praise seemed to spark in them.

Why else would I have returned here, if not to meet them? asked Greg, who then continued: probably also to see the bullfinch again, the one that had so impressed me back then.

A sudden longing for my home city came over me. It was, after all, foreigners with whom I was sitting, in a foreign part of the world; but this feeling didn't last and soon dissipated.

I suggested to my guests that they stay for lunch.

No, said the twins smiling, they had to get back to work. Even Greg declined to stay.

I was glad to get rid of them before afternoon came.

The sunlight was dazzling when I brought the visitors

to their cars. I was the only one wearing sunglasses; the blazing winter sun seemed not to affect them. Before Greg got in the car, he gave me credit cards so that I'd always have all the money I needed. I told him the arrangement with Gesellius had been something of a nuisance.

I watched them depart. Then suddenly the car carrying the twins stopped again. Harry got out, or was it Tom, and came up to me. His gait was proud and commanding. No man walks that way, I thought.

Do you have any idea how well you're doing? asked the Mormon. He used the informal "du" with me, and, because he was speaking German, I thought I had misheard him.

I did *not* know, and kept silent.

It was you yourself who got the ball rolling, he went on. If you're of a mind to spend the rest of your life in blissful idleness—everything stands ready.

He got back in the car and they took off, slowly, as though still waiting for something. For a moment I wanted to run after them and shout: Hey! Take me with you!

Even before the onset of afternoon, I was alone again.

I was in the garden when a feeling of forlornness came over me. I was standing in a grassy area looking at the hoarfrost on the short stems when suddenly I no longer knew whether I should be here or somewhere else, and asked myself the question where someone like me would best be harbored. Then came that faint, indefinite sadness that I had earlier taken for the feeling of loneliness. Then again, stronger, the forlornness and the disappearance of any trace of the ability to make a decision. How could I, so profoundly afflicted by the afternoon, ever have become mayor? I wanted to walk a few steps across the frozen lawn in order to hear the crackling of the hoarfrost under my shoes, but found myself unable to decide to do it. Now go, I told myself, take the first step, then it'll crackle and you can keep going, father and farther; just as Morler did it back then, you can do it too. Then again, the afternoon has its sweet side too, and it can be delightful to lose one's will. I was on a foreign continent, where a blue bird sang, now wistfully, now triumphantly, standing stock still.

Morler is occupying much too much space in your life, I thought, and then considered the possibility of committing myself any time I pleased to the care of the archangels. This thought gave me power, the grip of the afternoon loosened and I stepped onto the frozen lawn. Without a care, I walked across it, listening to the crackling produced by my steps. It was otherwise quiet.

I should've been happy, but in the meadows near the separating forest it would've sounded different. I remained standing and pulled up my pants leg to check the birthmark on my ankle. Then I went back into the house.

48

By the end of afternoon, I am often upbeat, even giddy. The idea came to me to keep Edna company that evening in the kitchen. I'll eat what you eat, I said to her, I'll share your supper. No fuss.

The subsequent food was very simple, just bread and cheese and sour pickles, besides beer. Everything tasted very good. But we couldn't get a conversation going.

Are you poor, Edna? I asked after a while.

Not at all, she replied, almost insulted.

I was still feeling the giddiness.

On the isle of America /

Gorgeous girls abound hurrah /

Pick me out the prettiest /

Take her home and count me blest ...

I'd recited it in German, and Edna looked at me uncomprehendingly.

Those are children's sayings, I said.

She asked me to translate, but I was ashamed.

She said I was too alone in the lonely house. Even so, I best not go with the archangels—I was too young for that.

If you were to decide about the rest of my life, I said, grown tired of beer, of winter, what direction would you give it?

She said I should do good with my wealth.

Yes, yes, I said and stood up. I'd sounded a bit harsh, so I added: Yeah, maybe I should do that. But then I said upon leaving the room: I wanted to have people come here, women included.

She figured that, nodded the cook. Herr Wilhelm did that too. She wished me a good night.

I, however, went outside, walked across the frozen grass that glistened in the moonlight (it was a full moon), took a stroll under the old trees that belonged to me, listened to the nocturnal animals as they cried out and watched them flit across the landscape that belonged to me. From here, the Grissmann House struck me as small and trifling as it stood there in the moonlight. Indeed, so unremarkably did it stand there, covered in silver, that it nearly moved me. In that house my predecessor had died, and I had become rich. In that house, under the influence of wealth, I had gone from being a left- to a right-handed person.

But I could have both, I thought, as I once again stood on the staircase outside, the replica and the museum!

Edna wants to invite guests for me. She said so this morning when she brought breakfast. She handed me a book from which I could choose. I perused the album. It contained pictures of people I didn't know. They all lived nearby, anyone could get here in forty-five minutes. But, according to Edna, the album was old and the people in it had grown older. In recent years, Herr Wilhelm had grown tired of visitors.

I drank the chocolate she brought me. What sorts of guests were they? Friends of Wilhelm?

She said they were of German descent, with roots in Wilhelm's old home region. But only one among them continued to come here on his own. All others were paid for their visit.

Choose some of them, I said, they're strangers to me! And no more then five, please, since it'll be an adjustment for me after these lonely days.

Edna nodded and left the room. I was alone in the Blue Room, drinking chocolate at the window I'd opened, listening to the bullfinch. The winter sun shone in warming me, cold air streamed in and cooled me off. This evening guests would be coming. For now I enjoyed the solitude. What, I thought challenging fate, could be more beautiful than this moment?

The guests arrived at seven o'clock. They'd come by car, one by taxi. The sun had gone down, the night had drawn near and you could see the headlights of the vehicles early on in the dark landscape.

The number had grown to six people: A married couple in middle age had brought their daughter along, a young woman in her early twenties. Added to them were a man and a woman around forty, who did not belong to each other, and an older man. He had come by taxi.

Shortly before the guests' arrival, I had paged through their dossiers but then decided I'd prefer to let myself be surprised.

The older man and the married couple knew each other from earlier visits, and after we had introduced ourselves to one another—we were all standing in the dining room, glasses in hand—they began to chat about their former visits here. No one was shy; but, I thought, why should that surprise you: after all, these are experienced guests who know how to handle themselves.

After a while, the young woman with whose visit we hadn't reckoned came up to me: Should she talk about herself or I about myself? She smiled at this. Her white, even teeth reminded me of Britta. Lorna was blond too, and, like Britta, had a slightly turned-up nose. Both had blue eyes, but Lorna's eyes were American, that is, calm and relaxed, so that one could gaze into them for a long while; I could not long endure Britta's gaze, nor she mine, so that the gaze one focussed on the floor or to the side was more often than not necessary to recover from the gaze of the other.

It was a pure delight to converse with these cultivated, witty people over an outstanding dinner, people who were tactful enough to keep their host from sensing all too sharply his own inadequacy to the fine art of conversation, of lively discussion. They fielded my awkward remarks, applied a veneer of brilliance to them, fed one another lines across the table, upon which Edna placed the most delectable dishes.

In the beginning I just let myself be entertained, but then my ambition was aroused and I came upon the idea of talking about the theories and views of my former teacher and mentor, Krautmann.

I said that only twenty percent of a person, thirty at most, displayed itself in interaction with others, in social exchange. The rest of the personality remained in the dark, in conversation with itself, lurking in the shadows of thought and feeling, invisible like the major portion of an iceberg; even when one wished, one could offer friends, loved ones, children, no more than twenty percent of oneself. That, I said, was the thesis of my teacher, Professor Krautmann, to whom I had much to be grateful for.

My guests had just been chatting about opera and death.

There was a lull in the conversation, during which everyone considered what I had just said; then Edna came in, cleared the table and left to fetch the next course.

This, I thought, is not the Grissmann House; it's only a knock-off. I'd almost forgotten that. And perhaps this moment was the first occasion on which I wished that neither one of them existed: not the museum and not its copy.

This Krautmann must've been an interesting man, said Lorna finally as she smiled at me.

The older man at the other end of the table had been silent the entire evening. He struck me as sullen, and I considered asking Edna to tell him he was free to leave. This man Krautmann, I continued, had been working on a typology of all people, of the entire human race. According to Krautmann, there were only a few types of human being, and these he was bent on classifying once and for all! And darn if she didn't remind me of another girl, I remarked, smiling at Lorna.

I watched the old man's face darken more and more.

And me? asked Lorna's father, which type was he?

I looked at him, and he moved his head in a way that reminded me of someone else I had known. But I couldn't think who it was.

She, however, I said, turning to my table-mate, bore a slight resemblance to my former wife, who had left me.

The older man jumped up and pointed his finger at me.

What's the problem? I cried out, what do you want from me?

Everyone was staring at me.

Go to the archangels, I thought, there you'll have nothing more to do with people.

My guest was still standing there, but a change had come over him.

It had been a delightful evening, he said, but now he must take his leave and never again be at my disposal as a guest.

Now he's in the vestibule, I thought, now Edna is pressing the money into his hand.

We carried on with our chitchat, a cheery dinner party, touching again on Krautmann's theses, then switching topics to sports and later to morality and justice.

I, however, couldn't help but dwell on the guest who had left: Now he's waiting in the driveway for the taxi; now he hears it coming; now he's getting in and giving the address … The taxi drove off and I lost him.

49

The guests have left. Once again I'm sitting in the room of the denier, where I also have my bed set up now. I don't use most of the rooms of the large house. Outside the window, moonlight, yellow in the sky, blue on the snow.

I'd wanted to ask Lorna to stay; perhaps she had expected it. It would have been nice to have the stimulating evening fade out this way, but my thoughts were with the guest who had left earlier, and so I limited myself to asking her as she left if we could see each other again.

Yes, we could see each other. She smiled and held my hand longer than necessary—we stood in the hallway like this, the other guests, including their parents, having already been escorted to the entrance by Edna.

She's quite different from Britta, I thought, but then immediately began to ruminate again over the question whether my remarks on Krautmann's theses had so infuriated the old man, and Lorna had joined the others. No sooner was she out the door than I had to recall to mind how beautiful she was.

A fox darts across the snow. I see him clearly since I've stepped to the window and the moon is bright. He's carrying something in his mouth, but I can't tell whether it's a bird or a mouse.

Later in bed I awoke with a start, just after falling asleep, and it was clear to me how it all fit together. I got up and woke Edna.

I asked her if she had the address of the guest who had left early.

Yes, she answered, drunk with sleep, she had the professor's address. In her pajamas, with her hair all tangled and her make-up removed for the night, she looked like a witch.

I told her to call for a taxi.

The taxi came, the driver got out and Edna approached him.

He wants to go to the professor's farm.

The cabby reminded me of a cowboy, lean and buff, and, as we rode in silence through the snow-covered, moonlit landscape, I saw his cowboy hat on the rear shelf. We turned off the road and drove along an unpaved path to a farmhouse that stood small in the moonlight next to a towering barn. Light still burned in one window.

Who is this professor? I asked, as the cab braked before the front door.

An outsider, the man answered, but he's been living here for a long time. He says his name is Troutman, Forellenmann, but nobody believes that's his real name. He used to breed trout, but then gave it up.

I asked him to wait till I came back.

No one forbids a rich man to visit him, even after midnight.

I rang the doorbell, which was new and seemed ill-suited to the neglected house—just generally, the moonlight with its silvery glow made the house look beautiful and well-maintained, but close-up you could see how shabby it was.

Footsteps approached the door. They shuffle a bit, I thought, but you still sense in them the energy of earlier times.

So you've found me at last!

He said this in German, even before opening the door, and so it was easy to recognize the voice that had held us in thrall years ago. How could I possibly not have recognized it at the dinner party!

So it's you who's inherited Wilhelm's fortune.

The door opened, and I saw that he was not alone, that a woman was standing behind him, with an Indian face, a squaw, so I thought. The weak hallway light, but also the proximity of the woman, who was young, made him look older.

This was one of the most beautiful moments of my life, I said. I told him he could hardly imagine how happy I was to have found him. *On the isle of America*, I began to chant, wishing to recall for him our time together.

While I was speaking, the Indian woman had stepped in front of her man as if to protect him and now began to rain blows on me while cursing in a language I'd never heard before. Blows aimed at my face I could fend off—her kicks I evaded, as elegant as a dancer.

Krautmann said something to her, something brief, perhaps her name, and she calmed down.

She hates everything from my past, Krautmann said, even my native language. If I wanted to do him a favor, we should speak English with each other.

The Indian woman was strong; it had cost me energy to restrain her. And she too was out of breath, her dark face grown darker from the effort; it was as if we had made love and now had to recuperate.

He's been raising trout, I thought, and now he's living with an Indian woman on a rundown farm in a remote spot in the eastern USA. I could feel the envy of this strange destiny creeping into me. Then too, I thought, how could it be any different with Krautmann; even in his decline, his farm is beautifully and superbly situated, just as a certain charisma continues to envelop the man himself. And yet there was something else, something about him I hadn't noticed before, something I hadn't wanted to admit to myself.

Krautmann, I said, don't you want to go back? I'll build you an institute, one that would dwarf the old one!

He didn't answer.

I was ashamed, I added in English in order not to upset the Indian woman, not to have recognized him earlier in the Grissmann House, but everyone believed him dead. I said I was happy to see him alive.

Suddenly the Indian woman made a gesture, and, although I could see that it wasn't all right with

Krautmann, I followed her into the house. How plain, how humble everything looked!

Yes, I'm a poor man, the professor acknowledged, noticing my curious glances; everything I had has been consumed by the cursed trout, and now I'm reduced to playing the guest of rich people!

He laughed.

As I looked around the living room without inhibition—a fire was going in the fireplace and the Indian woman had brought beer which we drank straight from the bottle, I thought I detected a plan behind all this penuriousness. That's just it! I thought and had to smile: A museum was to be established, one concerning itself with Krautmann.

Neither of us felt like talking, and I respected the mood, picturing to myself in silence the refounding of the institute and Krautmann's return to his hometown.

The fire had burned down some, its acute heat giving way to a milder, more even one which made me sleepy. Before long the Indian woman had brought several bottles for each of us. A clump of blazing logs collapsed in the fireplace, scattering sparks everywhere, and it grew even darker; we had not turned the lights on.

They're kissing, I thought, but I could see from the corner of my eye how Krautmann began to knead the Indian woman's breasts.

I asked whether I should leave, mentioning I could come back tomorrow.

The couple didn't hear me, just as if I weren't there. Krautmann unbuttoned the woman's blouse, the better to get at her breasts, and in the weak light of the fire I saw that her nipples were darker than those of European women.

The light dwindled further and further; only the crackling of the logs and the noises made by the couple could be heard; then the embers collapsed even more, and, just as with stars, the collapse caused the fire to flare up anew, and so it was that I saw the Indian woman's pubic hair. Then, with her help, the man penetrated her. I turned my gaze away.

A saying of Krautmann's about homeland and homelessness occurred to me. Quietly I stood up and left the house.

Outside, the moon had disappeared and a vast sky of stars arrayed itself above me. I thought about space and time and couldn't get past square one. Still and all, I thought, beauty abides.

Next to his cab stood the taxi driver smoking. He'd added the cowboy hat to his getup. The motor was running.

50

I'd intended to drive back over to Krautmann's place as soon as the next day. But after breakfast I strolled into the park instead, pondering the question where in my hometown I would wish to build the new institute, and whether it should resemble the old one.

In any case, the director's new office should be larger than the old one—though we thought even the old one was large. Gesellius had often joked that the director's office had squeezed the assistants' offices together, that they used to be larger, that it would at some point crush all our rooms.

But would Krautmann, as I had come upon him, feel at home in that kind of spacious director's office; is he not simply—and here I had to consider his sex act with the Indian woman without regard to my presence—unfit to head up a new and larger institute? He had bred trout and come a cropper, I thought, but somehow I felt that it had been me who'd failed at breeding trout. My past as a traveling lecturer came to mind.

The Grissmann House was visible in the distance; it belonged to me. How beautifully the snow lay upon the park's trees and meadows! A bullfinch sat on the snow, a patch of blue against the white.

Even back then, we, that is, Krautmann and his assistants, had been fiercely attacked by the academic wing. They're afraid, Krautmann had said, afraid that we homeland researchers are bringing something monstrous to light.

Lorna called, Edna said at lunch. Lorna was feeling just splendid, she wanted me to know. And there was another call. It was Morler asking if I were here. She said no, as I had wished. He didn't believe her, however.

I was in the park indulging in daydreams, I said laughing. I did this mindful of the fact that, for someone like me, there were no daydreams, since there was hardly anything I could not manifest in reality.

And as far as Lorna was concerned, I said, if she should call again saying she was feeling splendid, let her come over! Then we'd have a wedding.

That was just a joke, I added, noting Edna's astonishment.

Then came the afternoon. Everything was for nothing, the locating of Krautmann pointless.

51

I've offered Krautmann money to tell me why he disappeared, why he left us in the lurch. We're sitting in the denier's room and Edna is serving us tee. I've had Krautmann brought here in a taxi. It's early evening; soon I'll be turning the lights on.

I asked him why he left us in the lurch.

Instead of answering, however, he starts prattling on about the trout that ruined him, and I apologize: I should have asked the question without consideration of money, as is customary among friends.

He almost looks the way he used to, tall and slim, but soon he'll be gaunt and his full head of hair will turn gray.

I'm regarding him closely, as I was unable to do recently in the exuberance of having found him; yes, I can see how he enjoys sitting here over tea in this magnificent room, with a very rich man who admires him. Again and again he takes something from the tray of confections that Edna has set out.

He says he woke up one morning from restless dreams and was as if transformed. His love of homeland research and the institute: All that had fallen away from him, as though extinguished by sleep and dream. In the moment of waking, all of it had become a matter of complete indifference to him, replaced by a single thought: You are free.

The metallic quality of his voice that once inspired us so is gone. Its rasping edge had given way to a melodic, almost mellow tone.

I'm rich, so I can give free rein to my feelings, and so I admit that I'm somewhat disappointed in him. Also, he's at an age at which one should not be poor.

He went on to say that, with this thought of being free, he left his house and went to America. After a number of years it was too late to go back. He then asked if I was serious about reestablishing the old institute.

It would be named after him, the Wilhelm Krautmann Institute, I answer, and can see his happy smile in the diminishing light.

He doesn't thank me. The Krautmann of yore wouldn't have either. The present one, however, on the verge of gauntness as he is, should perhaps do so.

Krautmann then asked me if he was to lead this institute. Is that the way I had envisioned it? And wasn't I concerned about frittering away my money? Am I to be the head honcho again with you assistants obeying me?

He laughed and we raved about the good old days, and more and more he came to resemble the passionate scientist who was so adept at inspiring youth with his subject—but then he said something, and once again I knew that our relationship had turned upside down:

He said it did him good to be sitting here.

Yes, I even despised him a little, his age and his poverty.

Edna came in to clean up and turn the lights on.

Now I observed him again closely. His eyes had lost the glow of the idealist; he sat there in the armchair slightly stooped, his hand reaching erratically for the teacup. I should throw him the hell out, I thought. Do I really want to place a resplendent institute at the disposal a failed fishmonger?

He asked whether he might not have a glass of the good cognac.

He said this to Edna, who was on her way out; she looked at me, and I nodded.

He said his wife was feeling homesick for the reservation. He'd wanted to live there with her, but it didn't work out. He'd learned her language, very quickly, languages were no problem for him, not even the Indian languages, but the more he understood during his weeks on the reservation, the clearer to him the hatred became that was coming at him.

I asked him if they hated him because he was a white man.

Yes, Krautmann answered. And if he were to become head of the institute in his hometown again—he had not as yet made up his mind—his wife would go back to the reservation.

By the way, I'd wear a very beautiful suit, he continued, then wondered whether the suit would be made in his hometown. There was a shop there, he said, that made such suits. And you? he asked abruptly. May I use “du” with you? Will you go back to collecting children’s verses?

Yes, that was the plan, I said. And, as if he were Armbruster, to whom I could entrust anything, I told him about the great alternative to this plan: about the archangels and their bliss. There were drugs, I said, unimaginably expensive drugs, drugs the ordinary person would never even set eyes on. I didn’t know their effect, I said, but anyone who’s taken them even once thenceforth wished for nothing further in life, so I’ve been told. And, accordingly, the secret name of this drug was “God.” I could spend the rest of my life in a state of bliss in some beautiful, solitary spot, even if under permanent medical supervision.

I paused. Krautmann’s sharp-edged loser’s face had softened; there was nothing in it to remind one that trout had been this man’s ruin.

He’d heard of it, he said finally. On the Indian reservation. He himself had considered it superstition, superstition of the natives. They claimed that, without their knowledge of fungi, the knowledge that had been stolen from them, “God” would never have been developed.

Krautmann sat up straight, his head moved towards me, closer, and he looked me in the eye.

If he recommends it, I thought, you’ll do it.

What I wouldn’t give to be in your position, he said impassively!

He leaned back again and turned his face away.

I could see he was suffering. Perhaps it was his heart's desire to be happy forever living apart from all men; perhaps this dream had ripened on the reservation where he was hated; perhaps it was a consolation for him to believe that this drug did not exist. But it did exist. He would never live to enjoy it. I changed the subject.

I told him I'd had problems making decisions, my whole life, and now with the inheritance a boundless power of decision had fallen to me. I could do almost anything! That oppressed me. A while ago, I confessed to him, I had wanted to throw him out, but my inability to decide caused me to founder. But now, I said, I was happy to chat with him.

Edna knocked and I called her in. In a large brandy glass on a tray she was carrying the cognac. She placed the glass in front of Krautmann, who sat there in a state of collapse, his face buried in his hands. We both listened closely to detect whether he was crying, but could hear nothing.

I signaled Edna to leave the room.

Georg, Krautmann said after she left the room, Georg, my old assistant! If you go back, Georg, take me with you! Please take me with you! Take me with you!

He looked at me and shook his head with a sad and beautiful gesture. Rembrandt could have painted him that way.

Later, I said, later, adding, if I did end up going back, I'd take him with me.

52

I've given Krautmann money to avert the impending foreclosure sale of the trout farm. He visits me more frequently now, but he comes alone, since, as he never tires of telling me, his wife hates everything about his earlier life.

When he comes in the taxi paid for by yours truly, we've developed a ritual that would've fit nicely into our time at the institute: Krautmann gets out, I'm already standing there in the open doorway, and Krautmann calls: "Five minutes before the world was made …", which I must answer with: "I shuffled across a potato glade …" Then we go into the house and play chess, or I lead him around the building and give mini lectures on the Grissmann family. Krautmann himself knows little about it because, although it falls within his field, it didn't interest him at the time. Of all the sayings I've ever collected, by the way, Krautmann likes this one about the potato glade best; actually, it's the only one he's retained.

Soon it'll be spring; then we intend to travel to the hometown together and look for a piece of property.

Edna has advised me to hire bodyguards, and when I told Krautmann about it on a walk in the park—the snow is gone—his face darkened.

He said he used to dream of being so important that he required bodyguards, armed, beefy thugs who would throw themselves in front of him to take a bullet; now, however, he continued laughing, he could only swallow his envy over the fact that a mere assistant had achieved such status.

Oh please, it means nothing to me, I responded crossly, annoyed by his envy, and listen, Krautmann, I said, put a lid on your jealousy so we can continue to get along.

Look here, Georg, he answered, the first blossoms of spring! But, getting back to the previous subject, he bent down, plucked a white American flower unknown to me and pinned it to the lapel of my coat: He would recommend Indians to me, tight-lipped, dangerous fellows; his wife's relatives did this sort of work, her brother included. By the way, he said, that was the Indian flower I was now wearing.

I would gladly entrust myself to Krautmann's leadership, as in the old days, but he's not up to it, he can no longer lead. He is a broken man, it goes without saying.

A broken man, I say to him; what is that anyway, a broken man?

He shakes his head and says: When you are one, you know it.

Krautmann eats a lot when he comes for lunch, which is frequently the case these days. I let him do as he pleases, in fact, I even encourage this near-gluttony by having Edna prepare dishes from the old country. He excuses himself saying that there's nothing like this on the farm here and he doesn't eat much there anyway, as he continues to take helping after helping.

Soon it'll be afternoon and I doubt that Krautmann can be of any help to me then. Wouldn't it be better, I wonder, to be alone then or together with Lorna. The trip with Krautmann hangs over me like a dark cloud in these moments. I have, by the way, decided not to put up a new building—too much time would be lost doing that.

Krautmann, don't you sense too how the afternoon is encroaching? I asked him recently. But he didn't understand the question at all, my attempts to explain fizzled out, and he took yet another helping.

I don't care for the denier's room anymore. I told Edna to put clean sheets on the deathbed in the Red Room. The bed there was wider, I said, the spring firmer—Edna smiled as I said that and lowered her head to keep me from seeing her knowing smile. And she's right: I'm playing with the thought of inviting Lorna and it would be for an afternoon. Would her proximity be likely to lessen the weight of the afternoon? Perhaps she might help me to conquer the afternoon.

Lorna called again, Edna says, as I eat dinner with her in the kitchen.

What will she expect from me when she comes, Edna? Do I have to give her money as I did to the guests?

Edna shakes her head.

Soon I'll be leaving all this behind me, I think. I have

found Krautmann and will reestablish the institute. And I fantasize how I'll go around to schools and kindergartens preserving what would otherwise be lost.

53

I called Lorna after my chat with Edna and asked her if she'd like to come for lunch the next day. Her voice sounded as if she were already in bed.

I asked if I'd woken her up. Her voice sounded so tired, I said, and it occurred to me that it could be sadness, not fatigue.

I repeated my invitation and she remained silent.

Finally she said that in order to visit me at noon, she would have to take off work. Did I remember what her work was?

I couldn't recall and asked myself if that had come up in the conversation the other evening.

Teacher, no—librarian?

Yes. But if I wished, she could get off work.

That would be delightful, I said. In the evening I'm often melancholy, you know, and prefer to be alone.

She said she'd take off tomorrow and come visit me. At noon, if that was all right.

I answered that there was one other thing I had to mention, something that might make her wish not to come. I was going to Europe the day after tomorrow, perhaps forever, which meant that the shadow of departure might be cast over our rendezvous.

She didn't answer. I heard her breathing like someone who calls up strangers and doesn't announce himself, just breathes.

Then she'd rather not come, she said, and thanked me for the invitation.

We hung up.

I'd already gone into the Red Room when Lorna called back and said she'd come after

54

The next day I stood in the open doorway, in the place I stand when Krautmann comes visiting, gazing out upon the trees in the park. A green fluff is beginning to show on their branches; soon the bullfinch will be able to hide in the maze of their foliage.

Tomorrow I travel to Europe with Krautmann.

I stretched out my hand to test the falling rain. I no longer knew what I wanted from Lorna, and I was jolted when I heard her car from a distance in the quiet, rainy air.

It was a red European car, small by American standards, and I was surprised at how fast she drove, how close to the door she drove up and how sharply she braked: Gravel went flying, a pebble struck me painfully in the chin. As she got out, I saw she was wearing the same dress as recently.

The melancholy she had admitted on the phone seemed gone and she smiled at me.

You drive like a race car driver. Not like a librarian.

She said she had driven in amateur races, but that she wasn't talented enough to make it a profession.

Sometimes, I answered, it seemed to me as though I were the only one able to realize his dreams.

I had not given Edna any special instructions on what she should serve us for lunch; I'll leave it to you,

I said. Now for the first dish she brought in oysters. Lorna had to laugh.

What was she laughing at? I asked, though I knew well enough.

At first she didn't want to come, Lorna said, because I was leaving the country tomorrow. But partings were part of life; again and again one had to take one's leave.

I told her she was a person who often vacillated between exuberance and melancholy.

She asked me whether I too did not know such vacillations.

I said since I'd become rich they'd subsided. But it occurred to me that there were those damned afternoons, both before and after, with their gentle dread that would envelop me like cotton and threaten to suffocate me. After dinner, I thought, maybe you'll tell her about them.

If someone were to put a race car at your disposal, or someone were to set you up with a racing stable, would you be happy then?

Not another word! she replied angrily. What the hell good would it be if she had a car but could only lose with it?

Fine, I said, so let me talk about myself. Tomorrow I'd be traveling to Europe with Krautmann, I told her; we would be establishing a new institute in my and his hometown, an extension of the one Krautmann used to head up that conducted research on homeland. My intent was to start over again as an assistant there; I was looking forward to it.

I'd become carried away with what I was saying, and saw that I was infecting Lorna with my enthusiasm, her tight-lipped face relaxing. However, my enthusiasm began to cause me anxiety; indeed, I didn't care at all for this enthusiasm, and I was plagued with doubts as to whether it wasn't feigned. Everything struck me as unreal, and the fact that I wanted to exert myself to please a woman overwhelmed me. The archangels crossed my mind.

Edna brought in the next course.

This, she said, was a fish dish from the south. Creole style, one would say today, though in earlier times, or so she'd heard, one would've called it peon style.

We nodded, tasted and praised it. She left the room and we ate. At which point—as though magic were in play—we suddenly fell into a condition of mutual infatuation.

I reached for her hand.

She said I had a tiny drop of blood on my chin. She stood up, came around to me with her handkerchief, acting as though she wanted to wipe it, and kissed me.

She told me not to forget her while I was in Europe celebrating triumphs with my institute; and, if that didn't work out, I could come back to America; she would have a husband and children by then, but we would drink coffee together and think about the afternoon when we were in love for a couple of hours.

She moved me, but aroused me as well, and I led her into the Red Room.

When we began, I didn't compare, as I otherwise often do, nor did my vivid imagination transform her automatically into a different woman.

It wasn't until very late that I noticed it had become afternoon. I hadn't even noted its coming, which is worse than its presence. But then, who gave a damn about the afternoon! Every impulse to talk about it had left me.

Saying goodbye was easy, as though she were only leaving to fetch something and would be right back.

I stood in the doorway. Lorna drove off, motor howling, wheels spinning. A lady racer. A bullfinch was spooked and flew up screeching.

The next morning I said goodbye to Edna.

55

Krautmann was waiting for me in front of the trout-farm residence. He had only a gym bag with him. I too traveled with minimal luggage. On such a spring morning, one should leave on a journey without luggage. Next to him stood the squaw and, slightly apart from her, a man in front of a fully loaded pickup. He was an Indian; his very posture, his way of waiting, betrayed the fact.

I got out of the taxi hesitating to draw nearer, however, because Krautmann had just taken his wife into his arms.

The sun rose above the barn roof and blinded me. Then, as I shielded my eyes with my hand, I could see that nothing had changed. The two of them stood there embracing, while the Indian, immobile, a freeze frame, stood in front of his truck.

I didn't know how they would receive me. Now the sun stood behind an enormous plane tree and I could see the farm in its total squalor. Maybe I should buy it, I thought, and breed trout here till it was time for something else.

The woman left his embrace, then went back and kissed him. Then she got into the truck. Krautmann wiped his eyes.

Good, I thought, it hurts but he can't stay here, and the reservation is also out of the question.

All the signs for departure were there, and as the truck started up, I turned to Kaufmann, took his bag and said: Off we go, Wilhelm, off we go to brave new deeds! He sure is gaunt, I thought. Soon I'd be gaunt too.

Off we go, I said as I slapped Krautmann on the shoulder. Off we go! Off we go! I couldn't stop saying it.

Jubilation. Such a rare feeling! You might experience it at sporting venues, or in politics, but rarely in everyday life. And, I asked myself, is it in accord with your situation? How often it is that feelings do not conform to reality, that we're happy in situations that do not warrant it—or unhappy when there is no good reason. This gap, said Armbruster—or was it Krautmann, the old Krautmann, not the trout-Krautmann, or Troutmann, sitting next to me now—this gap would grow larger and larger.

Beneath us the Atlantic. I sit at the window, amazed as I still am by the miracle of flight. Yes, jubilation. And I catch myself thinking that I really don't want to get there but would rather stay here, up in the air.

Krautmann is asleep, two seats away, the seat between us empty, and as I tear my gaze away from the ocean, I see that sleep has rejuvenated him.

It is not until we go home that home is realized, according to the old Krautmann; if you never leave home, it remains something inchoate, something it doesn't pay to contemplate.

This was my second homecoming since becoming rich. And although the first one was not so long ago, and I could still remember most of it—still, my memory of the protagonist was blurry, and I wondered who it was that had experienced it all. The sea and jubilation, that'll have to do.

Krautmann is talking in his sleep, so I take his head and position it more comfortably, as I pull up his first-class blanket which has slipped down on him. He's had too much of the complimentary champagne. I, on the other hand, am already suffering from the disease of the rich, who can afford anything but no longer give a damn.

Europe is now coming into view, the uniform shapelessness of the ocean gone, and as I behold the landmass beneath me, a faint anxiety seeps into my jubilation. Jubilation or anxiety, I must decide. Jubilation.

I think of Antaeus as we slowly descend and soon enough reach the earth. The giant who acquired superpowers whenever he touched his mother, the earth. He was invincible. But then Heracles came, lifted him up off the ground and strangled him in the air.

Antaeus, I say to myself, and Krautmann is awakened by it.

End of Story

56

I hadn't given a thought as to how people would receive me in my hometown, hadn't thought about how things should proceed; I had only indulged my jubilation and surrendered myself to the future with a giddiness typical of many who have come to riches owing to no merit of their own.

I was greeted with hatred and mistrust, and it was all I could do to convince Krautmann, my trophy, that that was normal for someone returning home, that the general mood would soon turn and people would accept us with open arms.

We'd arrived late at night, and at the Krone only the prince and regency suites were still available. The evening clerk was a very old man, tall and gaunt. He eyed me as if I looked familiar but he had forgotten who I was, and as I was filling out the registration forms—Krautmann had taken a seat in an armchair in the lobby and was struggling to stay awake—a flash of anger crossed the old man's face, after which he was again attentive and friendly. Indeed, he must've noticed that his tinge of anger had not escaped me and he excused himself, saying he'd mistaken me for someone else. He'd mistaken me for someone with exactly the same name as me.

The light in the lobby was muted; a weak lamp glowed above the reception desk; it was two-thirty.

Between the dozing Krautmann and the old evening clerk, I was feeling as though I'd only been away from here for a short time.

The prince suite? The regency suite? I exclaimed. Exactly what we were looking for!

My voice was almost swallowed up by the muted light, by the heavy drapes fronting the windows, while the clerk's raspy whisper, like the stage-whispering of an actor, was all too clear and hurt my ear.

Who's the prince? Who's the monarch here? The old man smiled, carrying the two key cards one in each hand, changing them faster and faster from one hand to the other the way scam artists on the street do with their little hat game. With a deft move I swiped both cards from him, surprising him in the act.

I'm the prince, I'm the monarch here, I said. He stood there looking at his own empty hands, astonished and disappointed.

So it's you who are the mayor who played us all for fools!

I said nothing. He acted as though he hadn't made that last remark.

Later, I thought, we'll both write this scene off to the late hour, to the hour between wolf and dog, to jet lag. A sleepy page brought us and our luggage to the suites. I gave Krautmann the prince suite, the more expensive one. Morler had occupied it for quite a while at my expense.

If we should fail to buy back the old institute building from the lawyers, I was thinking at breakfast as my gaze settled on the castle outside the window that loomed high above us, it'll be built anew up there.

Krautmann, what would you think of the castle?

But Krautmann has had the newspaper brought to him, has opened it to the local section and buried himself in it, and is now sighing and can't comprehend how long he's been away and all that has happened since.

The acting mayor should stay on, he reads half-aloud from a letter to the editor; he's a good mayor, unlike the other guy who left the city in the lurch.

The waitress brought fresh coffee.

First he wanted to look Gesellius up.

Do you want company? I asked him.

No, he wanted to speak with him alone, Krautmann answered.

The castle, I repeated, what would you think of the castle, Krautmann?

Sure, the castle's good, he answered. But I noticed his mind was somewhere else, no doubt already at Gesellius' office.

During our conversation, an overwhelming aroma of coffee had filled the breakfast room, the fragrance of the finest, most expensive coffee; the smell was almost too much for me. The best things are often too strong, I thought; one must build up a tolerance for them.

Suddenly Krautmann stood up and was already halfway across the room on his way out.

You'll find him in the bank at the Schimpfeck Mall! He's the bank manager! I called after him. He turned towards me and nodded, bristling with energy.

The waitress came and poured me a refill, and when I thanked her, she asked with a smile: Are you the mayor who disappeared, who left us in the lurch?

Yes, that's me, I responded in the same airy tone.

57

I had called my mother from America. She was relieved to learn I was not dead. Back when I called her, I had not intended to return. It was the rediscovery of Krautmann that moved me to do that.

I walked up the narrow street of the old town and saw the museum standing before me. How beautiful its facade was, even though two smaller, insignificant houses sandwiched it and it didn't stand free in a park like the other one.

A group of tourists were streaming out the door, Asians, followed by my mother. They gave her tips and expressed their thanks.

I waited for the group to move away. How little my mother was next to the big building. For a moment I imagined how Krautmann was now seated in Gesellius' office, perhaps in the same seat in which I had sat, and how they were talking about me and my project. A slight feeling as of afternoon came over me, and, in order to shake it, I stepped over to my mother and held her eyes closed from behind. She recognized me immediately and we hugged each other.

She said she had an hour and a half free till the next group. Let's go home and then you can tell me everything!

She reached for my hand as if I were still little; where are you going, I wanted to say, but then I remembered that we lived across the street.

The dining room table was set for two for coffee. Nope, she said and set a third place; she hadn't counted on me showing up, she was expecting a girlfriend. They met occasionally, she said, and would most often talk about me over coffee and cake. It was Ingrid, my ex-wife.

The doorbell rang and my mother went to answer it, but did not come back immediately, rather talking softly with the arrival.

We greeted one another like old friends, and I complimented Ingrid: on her green dress and how it suited her, on how well it went with her dark hair, which she was again wearing longer now than back then at the Cafe Völter. You know, you're courting her, I thought.

She asked me why I had taken off, why I'd fled.

I sat down, to encourage her and my mother to sit.

Oh, my candidacy, I said; that whole mayor business was just one of Morler's tactics!

They shook their heads over how lightly I was taking the matter, but sat down anyway.

Why did I come back and what did I want here? my mother asked finally.

I'm going to turn back the wheel of time, I answered. Just imagine, Ingrid! You were an assistant yourself at the institute. Krautmann, by a strange chain of events I've found Krautmann.

They stared at me incredulously.

Krautmann is here, I said, I've brought him back

with me; he's sitting in Gesellius' office at the bank right now! You too could join the team!

I gave a broad outline of my plan. My proposal seemed to rouse them. I finished talking and took the silence that ensued as confirmation of my inspiration.

People always spoke well of me, my mother finally said. They were prepared to forgive my leaving the city and its citizens in the lurch.

I felt as though I were exuding a faint human-monkey-smell, treacly and stale.

During the period of my absence, said my mother, the coffee klatches and the conversations about me had been more enjoyable.

Should I leave? I asked.

My mother took my hand: No, no, she was glad I was there. You too, Ingrid, right?

Yes. But she had to go now, my ex-wife answered.

My mother looked out the window. People were assembling in front of the Grissmann House.

Upon leaving Ingrid gave me her hand.

Bergius was back in the neighborhood, she said. The press of her hand was firm with nothing tentative about it, like that of someone who feels at home in his body. He was happy to be teaching Latin again.

It's getting to be time for me too, my mother said. And something else, Georg: When a man who has flopped comes back home rich and powerful, people fear his vengeance.

What? Oh, come now, vengeance? I cried.

Through the window I watched her lead the group into the Grissmann House.

58

From the museum to city hall is not far. The Grissmann House is the older of the two.

I still had time; Krautmann and I weren't scheduled to meet at the hotel for another hour. Good, I thought, go to the marketplace, have a look at the Renaissance facade of the city hall. I scarcely laid eyes on it and walked right in.

Whom did I wish to see, the concierge called to me from his stall.

The acting mayor, I heard myself say.

In that case he would have to see some ID.

I walked back and showed it to him. The man seemed taken aback and reached for the telephone. He was a man of my age, already bald, a pycnic type who sweated easily. You, on the other hand, consort with archangels, I thought.

The mayor was expecting me.

I climbed the stairs to the second floor. Here is where they wanted to honor me for having rescued a child from drowning—but I didn't want that. With the devil-may-care attitude of the man of means I rejected the honor.

The hallway was empty. But a woman stood in an open doorway gesturing to me, and as I walked towards her—*five minutes before the world was made* —she called to me by name. Herr Grissmann. Herr Georg Grissmann?

Fear not, I said, it's a friendly visit.

We all love the mayor; please don't hurt him!

She smiled, a smile right out of an old American film when people still believed destiny could be steered and controlled by sex-appeal.

She walked ahead of me to a door which stood open.

I'm not here to hurt anybody, I said behind her back.

Morler was sitting at his desk, bracing for the worst, yet calm. Just the way a mayor was supposed to look. Of all the mayors whose portraits hung on the walls, Morler came closest to the image of the ideal mayor. His bulk radiated peace, his serious facial expression authority.

I had no idea how to greet him.

So, this is what it comes down to, Morler said pre-empting me.

He gestured at a chair in front of his desk and I sat down.

Here is where he'd found his life's purpose, Morler said, more to himself than to me. He was born for this calling; and not only did *he* think so, but his co-workers as well, the whole city in fact. But now I was back and the whole business was finished.

I knew Morler well, so I could tell it was only with the greatest difficulty and self-control that he was able to maintain his official mayor's smile when he would've much preferred to break out in tears.

I don't want your office, I said. I'd only come back in order to re-establish the institute at which I had worked a long time ago.

What's the good of that, Morler replied. Since I was now back on the scene, I was mayor and he, as interim mayor, was legally bound to yield to me. But if I were to relinquish the office, a new election would be scheduled. He, however, not being a resident of the city, could not legally be a candidate.

Those last sentences had been forcefully articulated by the mayor, and the secretary craned her neck into the doorway.

Everything okay in there; need any help?

No, we're old friends, Morler answered bitterly, and she withdrew.

Something Gesellius once said to me came to mind. That I was a troublemaker, a disruptive element no one wanted to have around.

Then you do hate me? I asked.

Morler began to laugh, any trace of dignity having vanished from his face.

Hate was too big a word, he said finally. Without me he would never have been able to occupy this office. By the same token, he had been fearing my return.

I looked at my watch. How little time had passed since I'd entered city hall!

Something came over me, and I gazed into Morler's face as if it were far away, as if I were contemplating a distant mountain peak, a sunset. Suddenly I knew the future. Not mine, just Morler's, and I stood before the decision to announce it or not.

You will remain mayor, I said, the city council will pass an exemption. You'll be mayor, but then you'll become ill.

He didn't quite catch the last thing I said, Morler replied.

You'll be mayor, I repeated.

He nodded, and all tension drained from him. I, however, had already forgotten the end of the prophecy.

Morler, I said in a totally different voice, all visionary timbre having vanished from it, Morler, I want to tour the schools again, the kindergartens, the orphanages. And collect whatever the childlike souls have created to explain the world. I told him it was for this purpose alone that the institute would be re-established. Help me out with this! It would be of great benefit to him and the city.

Fine, count me in, he answered.

Morler! Where were you running to back then?

But the mayor is having none of that.

59

Everybody's joining in, each ready to have another go at it. I have infected them with my enthusiasm, with my plan: Gesellius, Ingrid, Krautmann, myself. Morler promises us total support, Armbruster will join us as soon as soon as his sentence is up.

And even if something akin to a sfumato adheres to our inspiration, a slight blurring of boundaries—nothing unusual with second efforts, once one has already experienced failure—so what! Britta will run our canteen, our cafeteria, once I locate her.

At our meetings—in the Krone's Green Salon—I let Krautmann do the talking. I discuss everything with him ahead of time. Sometimes at the beginning of his remarks his mind may still be lingering on his Indian woman, or on his trout—but then he catches himself, waxes enthusiastic, displays the old lightning flashes of insight.

I look around me and am happy. Ingrid no longer resembles the woman I rejected in the Cafe Völter; she is an Amazon. Gesellius no longer gives the slightest air of a bank manager: He's bursting with intellectual elegance.

We intend to try to acquire the Grissmann House for our new establishment, Krautmann announces.

This had not been agreed upon. It's Krautmann's idea, his alone, and while the waiter is serving coffee and water as noiselessly as possible, and for Krautmann beer, everybody's looking at me.

I don't answer immediately. Opposition from the city, the mayor, might possibly be broken with money. But that was not the main thing on my mind. This was the moment in which it dawned on me that wealth cannot only create but also destroy.

I looked into their faces and smiled. Yes, perhaps, I said. Most importantly, however, we should commence with our project.

60

The city council has approved the waiver for Morler. He is now the mayor. A former private detective is now running this city and is running it well. He is immune to blackmail, having scrupulously laid bare his shabby past life. Perhaps Morler is the big beneficiary of my wealth.

The next day we gave our press conference. Institute Director Krautmann was the main speaker, Gesellius seated next to him at the podium, "his right hand and former bank director." I myself was not present, sitting as I was over a beer at the Deutsches Haus. From Ingrid's reports and from the newspaper I learned that Krautmann had done very well.

One passage from the newspaper article had especially pleased me. To the question as to why he had disappeared back then and why the new as well as the former mayor had now also briefly disappeared, he appealed to the concept of coincidence and the fact that research into coincidence had always been one of our focus areas and strengths.

You could be happy, I had thought over my beer in the Deutsches Haus. Now, having read the newspaper and heard Ingrid's report, I thought so again.

I've visited Armbruster. To do so, I had to go to the neighboring city where the prison is located.

He thinks a great deal; you can see that about him. His head, already large and chiseled during his heyday as a professor, is now, since he's become gaunt, even more emphatically his dominant feature. Everything about him has become more gaunt; nose and eyes seem larger, and it strikes me that some sort of metamorphosis is imminent: into an owl-man or into a genuine philosopher.

For now, since he's in punitive detention, there's no officer hovering over us as we talk.

When I entered the visiting room, he was already sitting in his chair in prisoner's garb. His new owl eyes gave me a sharp look. Yep, he said without any greeting, that's just the way he had imagined the effect of wealth on my appearance and my character.

I was desperately curious to know what exactly he meant by that, how he thought I'd changed, but was polite enough to inquire first after his situation and his wellbeing.

No doubt he rarely received visitors, and so every conceivable thing instantly burst out of him: For the time being he had set aside work on his aesthetics; what interested him for the present was the phenomenology of imprisonment. Thus his next magnum opus would be called: *The Phenomenology of Imprisonment*. The experience of imprisonment in all its manifestations, all its varieties, was what he wanted to describe, and, since at bottom the whole world was imprisoned, it arguably amounted to a description of the world.

He smiled, sadly and maniacally, and although his main thesis was immediately evident to me, still he struck me as a little sad. The totally radical thinkers had always struck me as sad.

It was warm. The sun shone in through the barred window, a cheerful morning sun, and all of a sudden it was a matter of indifference to me what Armbruster had to say about my transformation through wealth.

And you, Georg?

Armbruster, how about …? I said, the visit almost over, as I could see from the big clock on the wall, how about "Homeland and Imprisonment!" When you get sprung, come to the institute!

As he squinted into the light, shielding his eyes from the sun's rays, I told him about my plans in quick order. He found everything satisfactory. The only thing he objected to was making the Grissmann House the new institute:

You're destroying the very tradition you aim to study!

Ah, Armbruster, how finely formulated that is, you've actually coined a phrase; but the luster of a sentence says nothing about its correctness. How weak, I pointed out, how feeble was the mind, was philosophy, when pitted against known facts!

I glanced at the prison clock. Our time was up. I got up.

It marches on, he said. Everyone knows it, no one stops it. Five minutes left.

We were silent and sat together; then the judicial officer came, a big, heavy-set man with a friendly face.

Armbruster got up and stood opposite me. We shook hands, he smiled a satisfied smile. An idiot's smile, I thought. I envied him.

To an outsider we would no doubt seem like men who were saying goodbye to each other for a long time.

Morler, I've made my choice. I want the old institute building.

Morler squirmed like an eel. It's presently occupied by the corporate lawyers, he pointed out. That's the university's jurisdiction, not the city's.

Then he should approach the responsible parties and offer a ton of money, I said, refusing to take no for an answer.

61

Early on I had given some thought to the relation between money and violence. And while even then a not quite crystal-clear connection seemed to me to exist between the two, I now experimented with thought games as to how I might avoid violence with my money. Something to think about later. This came some time later to my mind.

We're standing on a knoll in the middle of the city. Krautmann, Gesellius, Ingrid and I. From our commanding height, we look down on a Wilhelmine brick building. A cold wind is blowing. But we are protected from the wind by the detention center to our rear.

Morler isn't with us, and I have a feeling he won't be coming. He has to consider his popularity.

It's still early, the occupants are asleep, invincible in their cosseted dreams. Students are sleeping down there in their sleeping bags. In our house. They want to be corporate lawyers and make a lot of money in the future.

Why won't they vacate? They could move into new, larger, brighter rooms, much better suited to career and profession. Precisely what, with great tenacity, with the cunning of corporate lawyers, they demanded from me and were granted. Now they don't want it anymore.

We loved that ugly building down there and would like to love it again, but others too have now taken a shine to it, even referring to it with the word "homeland." I have satisfied all their demands, to no avail. The fact that it belongs to me means little to them. On the contrary, because it belongs to me, they think they have a claim to it.

Krautmann produces a silver flask. He takes a swig and offers it to us. Only Gesellius drinks. I observe the whole business precisely.

The sun goes up. Police vehicles arrive.

They move slowly, as if to torture me. Speed it up, I think. Blue light intermingles with the first sun rays.

Just then the heretofore darkened windows on the second floor are illuminated. That's where Krautmann's office was. Now they're taking notice, I think, now they're opening the zippers of their sleeping bags with that typical sound. Now they're hopping out in the belief that the world loves them. But some, not including me, hate them. Youth remains blissfully unaware of this.

The police announcement is heard, that everything must comply with the law. It's a woman's voice, high-pitched and assertive. Also, they should give up the building voluntarily.

Soon they'll all be wide-eyed. For one thing must be clear: Before you know it, the police will exit their vehicles and place the battering rams in position against the barricade at the entrance, and, whether the occupants believe it or not, the clearance equipment will be deployed.

The dark, powerful boom of the ram. On top of that, sirens; the police sirens and the strokes of the ram, audible far and wide in the thin morning air.

Why are we here?

We are witnesses, Krautmann replies to Ingrid's question. This too is homeland, he says, and we are witnesses.

He has a pair of binoculars. Only he among the four of us thought to bring binoculars.

Light now in all windows, and in the thin air also music, courage-boosting music.

Finally they're getting in, Gesellius says.

Krautmann hands me his binos. And I peer into the lit windows, observing the coeds as they cover their breasts. However, I, the owner, see their naked breasts, even if only through the glasses.

How many female police there are down there!

They've turned off the sirens; it's only the students' music that can still be heard. Then the officers are inside. The music stops.

They'll carry them out, says Krautmenn, for he knows the future.

As always, as in the past, we believe him. Even though he lost all his trout and left us in the lurch that time. Ah, I think, there's the lady journalist down there, the one who interviewed you after rescuing the child.

They've all sat down on the floor, arms interlinked, we can see that even without binos, but only Krautmann, who has the scope, can distinguish faces.

They're carrying them, says Krautmann, passing around the flask.

Now Ingrid and I also drink the at-first pungent then smooth pear brandy.

How bright now the house in which we had so many experiences. Now they're carrying the first ones out through the shattered door. They make themselves heavy. Limp as maggots, like cadavers they hang in the officers' arms. Some of them will later be rich, though not so rich as I am. Remember, they'll say, that was our wild period.

We see well, but Krantmann with his glasses sees everything. And now I hear him softly whistling as he looks through the lenses: the Beatles' song about the "Fool on the Hill."

Now a herculean student has knocked a lady cop to the ground, says Krautmann—accidentally, it seemed to him. Now she's gotten up and is using her club to beat him around the neck and shoulders.

We continue to watch for a while, though when we leave, there are still students in the house. Gesellius stays. He'll be getting the key when the whole business is over, the key to the shattered door. He'll bring it straight to me.

The rest of us, however, are splitting up: Krautmann wants to have his first coffee at Völter's, Ingrid's going back to Bergius' place, and I'm heading back to the hotel to catch up on sleep.

Hours later I woke up and didn't know where I was. This is a hotel room, I thought. Even before I could recall my whereabouts, I knew that I was rich. Only then did I remember the name of the city. I didn't need to check the clock: I immediately recognized the light that peeked through a crack in the curtains: It was afternoon. But there was something new. It had no power over me.

62

I was now generally hated in student circles, and, in order not to jeopardize the institute's future, I kept to the background and avoided public appearances.

Nor did I continue living at the Hotel Krone, since persons unknown had sprayed caricatures of me on the wall following the eviction; at night in the hotel garden someone set fire to a larger-than-life-size effigy of me.

I moved back in with my mother, and, completely different from my last stay, when I was popular, she was now suddenly proud of me because people hated me.

For instance, whenever she's approached at the butcher's or on the stairs on the subject of yours truly, she boasts to people about her important son: how I acquired an immense fortune, how I reestablished the institute, how, in Krautmann, I brought back to the city an eminent authority, the leading luminary in the field of homeland research, how, together with Krautmann, I introduced the idea of the two prongs of research: "homeland and misfortune" and "homeland and coincidence."

You don't have to give the tours anymore, I tell her, you can move into any villa on the most beautiful hill in the city. She shakes her head in astonishment—of all the ideas! She was satisfied with things as they were.

It must be said, however, that she never cared much about the stature of the Grissmann family!

But that's all changed, she answers herself, since through me the family has recouped something of its former luster—and at an institute that was so in debt to me I could certainly become a professor there.

And she takes my hand and presses it; and it's only because I'm rich that I'm able to tolerate the pressure her heart's desire puts on me.

Though the evacuation took place only recently, the new students are already streaming to Krautmann's lectures. Especially to "Homeland and Coincidence"; "Homeland and Misfortune" interests them much less. And as so often I fail to understand people: The one lecture is certainly good, very good, but still old hat, whereas the other is of a brilliance and depth Krautmann would never have been able to achieve without his failure in America.

And me? Tomorrow morning I'm scheduled to visit an elementary school; tomorrow afternoon I'm going to an orphanage.

63

It was my old grade school. I'd gone to school here in the eighties. At the time of my first surveys fifteen years ago, I had avoided it, since I couldn't recall ever having heard a children's saying in this school for monkeys. Matthias Christian Laffe—the school is named for this theologian and naturalist from the early nineteenth century, the street as well. All the pupils called it the school for monkeys. It was not until I'd become better acquainted with the history of the city through the tours that I learned something about him. Namely that he'd been the adversary of one of my ancestors, an adversary who, with ridicule and justified mockery, dragged every publication of this Grissmann through the mud.

Enough, I stood in front of this building from the seventies. To its left I recognized the schoolyard on which the new gymnasium was to be built. Morler gave me to understand that, if I assumed the total cost, it could be named after me. I replied that my relationship with my family was ambivalent; I would donate only half the cost and my name was not to be mentioned.

I looked at my watch, a cheap quartz watch I wore because I could afford any watch. It was nine-thirty. Right now, I thought, well before ten, the first students are streaming into the lecture hall to grab a seat for "Homeland and Coincidence."

It's spring, but cold. I'm lonely.

I pushed open the yard gate and walked toward the entrance with these small steps, the way I used to walk as a child, as a pupil. They should all be looking through the windows to see how a grown-up walks with such small steps! How they'd laugh.

Morler had notified the school of my appearance. The headmistress was somewhat younger and just a tad shorter than I, with bobbed blonde hair and energetic movements signaling decisiveness and ambition. One of these women, I thought, who are successful as well as attractive, who—and I looked down at their feet—wear high-heeled shoes even in the morning.

And you'll abide by the agreed-upon conditions?

We'd gone into the headmistress' office on the second floor, which I knew from early days; I'd often been sent to the headmistress. The furniture, of course, was now modern.

Yes, I answered. I would proceed as agreed upon.

Three children had come forward who they said were willing and in a position to offer me sayings; all three girls, not a boy in sight. I was limited to eight minutes per interview. If they got embarrassed, I was not to press them but had to let them go. The school had told the parents that I was supporting it with the construction of the badly needed gymnasium, so that, if I were permitted to interview the children, it would redound to the community. The meetings would take place here in the headmistress' office, on each occasion with a qualified teacher present, who, however, would remain somewhat in the background. Otherwise the child might possibly suffer embarrassment. At some point, it always, or almost always, came around to delicate subjects, the headmistress smiled at me.

We'd sat down at the table, the headmistress drumming lightly on the tabletop, and now I recognized that it was my little book that she was drumming on—she must have picked it up somewhere.

Now a long pause ensues. Finally she says I may proceed with the interviews if I wish.

Since becoming rich, it makes less and less difference to me to keep my mouth shut, so I did just that.

You have an interesting watch.

Yes, I answered politely, quite a cheap one, from Woolworth's, seven-fifty, battery included.

She laughed and crossed her legs.

She said she knew some children's sayings too, sayings that weren't in my book yet. What strange ideas the children would come up with regarding the reproduction of the race! That she observed time and time again in her sex-ed class.

While speaking those last sentences, she was not looking at me but at her wristwatch, a man's Swiss watch, an expensive brand.

She's looking at her watch, I thought casually, to see if there's enough time to get it on with a very rich man …

There was a knock on the door, and the secretary nudged a girl of about seven into the room. In the same moment, the bell for recess rang.

What fair hair the child had! What fair skin! I couldn't see her eyes as she was wearing dark glasses.

Her name was Lotta, the child said, extending her hand to me. Then she turned to the headmistress: Here I am, Frau Niedermeyer.

The headmistress seemed startled, as though yanked from a daydream. This is the homeland researcher, Dr. Grissmann, a scientist, she said.

She stood up and walked to the farthest corner of the room to avoid listening in.

The child was now standing in front of me; I'd turned my chair to face her, holding my cell phone between myself and the girl.

I told her it was all about preserving the things children had thought up for themselves, the ideas they had about the world and life.

The confidence with which the girl behaved reminded me of someone; I couldn't remember who.

Banana, limetta—on the corner stands a man
Banana, limetta—he lures the girls as best he can
Banana, limetta—he takes them home with him
Banana, limetta—he strips them on a whim ...

She paused and looked me in the eye: a dramatic pause such as the pros make in order to emphasize the importance of what is to come.

She said she didn't know any more but that she could sing and dance and had already appeared on TV.

"Sweet dreams are made of this ..."

Her bright child's voice, so different from the sadly

profligate voice of Annie Lennox, happy and optimistic, since the girl didn't understand the lyrics.

Thank you, that's enough for now, said the headmistress. If you don't know any other sayings, you can go to recess now.

The girl, however, was not of a mind to stop, feeling her oats as she now was, and continued singing, even beginning to dance, as if she had a huge audience.

Finally the secretary was called in to take the child away. The girl resisted, and as the secretary took her by the hand and dragged her out of there, she continued to sing.

During all this it came to mind who her behavior reminded me of: Helena's son. Perhaps, I thought, one day he and this girl will run into each other on TV, fierce rivals …

Banana, limetta. When the child was gone, the headmistress said she was sorry I didn't get much out of that. But anyway at least *that* children's saying was still around and kicking. There were two other girls still waiting outside, she said in her headmistress voice.

The next girl, even younger then the first, had lied. She admitted she didn't know any sayings and claimed the other girls had clammed up when it came down to it. She said they told her the sayings were secret.

The third pupil was a little Kurdish girl. She said she knew verses, and, in order not to disappoint her, I took down what she said in Kurdish. She gave a mischievous smile; the foreign language, Greek to me, seemed to me to suit children's verses very well.

The recess bell rang, the girl started at the sound and ran out.

That wasn't much, said the headmistress, adding she had nothing more to offer. Was I disappointed?

64

That afternoon at the orphanage things didn't go any better for me. The seven orphans who had volunteered knew nothing, or nothing new, most of them simply repeating: *Banana, Zitrone/ Limetta...* Still, I said thanks to each one, you've helped me a lot. How easily and without risk I could have expressed my anger! I was given enthusiastic support for my offer to modernize the dilapidated playground behind the house.

I should really come back, said the directress as I was leaving. Maybe next time even the stubborn ones would be ready to cooperate. And it was just the stubborn ones who were most likely to know such sayings.

People encounter me and pass me by like shadows.

On my way to my mother's, it occurred to me what the Athenians said about St. Paul as he preached Christianity to them: What is this rake trying to tell us?

That evening the institute came together at the Krone to celebrate.

When I left my mother's, she walked me to the door and held me back by my sleeve to have a look at me, even turning on the hallway light to inspect my face closely. She looked worried and I noticed, as my face mirrored this worry, a certain sadness.

Are you unhappy?

No, everything's A-OK, I replied laughing, and through the miracle of communication her face relaxed. After all, what did she know of my feelings, my moods! I didn't even understand them myself.

I had promised myself not to keep silent at our celebration and was silent anyway. I sat among the revelers like transparent smoke. Nothing had changed at the Krone; it is only we, so I thought, who had swum further down the stream of time.

In the old days, Krautmann had been a regular here. He would come here in the evening quite alone, as we assistants found out, and order capon, all alone at his table.

What's the matter, Georg, you spawn of an ancient, fallen house? Didn't your kiddies know any sayings?

Without waiting for my reply, he refilled Ingrid's wineglass.

Just a few, and those already known, I said to Gesellius. Krautmann wasn't listening to me. Gesellius nodded and tried to make a sympathetic face. But behind that lay the exuberant *joie de vivre* with which Krautmann had infected him.

I wanted to be alone for a moment.

When I came back from the restroom, Krautmann stood up and flung his arms around my neck: Guess what, Georg, I've yet to tell anybody about this! He said the Minister of Cultural Affairs was at his lecture today, was impressed, and promised the institute a windfall of public funds. We're rich and soon we won't be needing your money!

Krautmann was now totally off the rails: He embraced Gesellius and kissed Ingrid, even shoving his tongue in her mouth. (Oh well! They'd once had a brief affair anyway.)

Then he calmed down a bit. His exuberance had exhausted him. Everyone sat back down, avoided looking at one another and drank.

Happiness loud and quiet, I thought. As for myself, I was thinking about the stubborn ones whom I hadn't even seen. The stubborn ones, I thought, they're probably right. Why does everything have to be passed on? It may, after all, be plebeian to want to inform someone of something. With this thought my mood was elevated. Suddenly I was happy again about my wealth. A rich man can get up and leave any time he likes. All the best, Krautmann, all the best, Gesellius, all the best, Ingrid, all the best, Armbruster, and all the best, mother! And to you too, I'd almost forgotten, to you too, Morler, all the best!

And come back when he likes.

The food arrived, and although I still felt no appetite whatsoever, I ate as voraciously as everybody else.

65

Ah, to you too, Helena, all the best and even to your obnoxious son.

66

That takes care of everything.

67

Homeland is not just a matter of place and time. It can also be a condition. Krautmann himself is yet to realize that.

68

I was at the Krone one more time, sat at the table Krautmann had once sat at, and later Bergius and the others, and later still those of us from the institute.

I was lost in thought and, in my contemplation of past and future, had knocked over my full wineglass. The young lad who was my waiter was there on the spot, cleaning up the table and bringing me a new full wineglass. Not a trace of the afternoon. The wine glistened in the candlelight, unspeakably beautiful. And so I knocked the glass over again, intentionally. Not a trace of the afternoon.

69

One week later, two identical buildings burned completely to the ground on the same day, though at different times. The one in Europe at night, the other in America during the day. No one was injured.

Rumor had it that Indians were in the neighborhood of the fires. I heard all this at the airport.

70

My gaze overlooks the sea. The foaming crowns are easy to spot from up here. Their whiteness in the sunlight painfully bright. But I can't tolerate this brightness for long, so I walk over to the landward side of the floor and look over the green, fruitful land and off into the wilderness.

Today I received my first injection.

Soon I won't want to write anymore. The stronger this feeling of happiness, the more it demands my complete attention. According to the doctor, everything suggests that the bearer of such happiness will lose himself behind the feeling, and be devoured by his own feeling. He says he knows he shouldn't be saying this, his colleague is already giving him the evil eye. But he'll say it anyway because it moves him deeply: I am an astronaut for whom he has unlimited admiration. Even if I never come back.

I'll be given the reduced dose for three days to see if I tolerate it.

Five minutes before the world was made
I shuffled across a potato glade ...

Now, on the second day, I suddenly understand the meaning of these words. How clear and beautiful they are! and I'm amazed that I never grasped them before. Yet, when the doctors come, with an archangel among them, and I greet him joyfully as prelude to interpreting the verse's deeper meaning for him, I find I no longer want to, and I also know why: You don't want to, you no longer need to. And so we chew the fat, as if nothing's up. It's a treasure that cannot be shared.

The angel says there's nothing different about me.

And yet, I answer him, it's there.

71

I know that tomorrow it'll be too late for that; right now, however, there's one question that still interests me. And I want to have it answered before the answer becomes a matter of indifference to me tomorrow:

Where would Morler have gotten to? Where did he want to go? Where would he be now if I hadn't stopped him?

I told them to keep the Learjet on standby, with a helicopter at the landing site.

72

The location was quickly found, even though it was by an improbable coincidence that I recognized the road and, as we flew alongside it, the place as well. I had the helicopter pilot land and got out. Even the season was alike: Just this way and no other did the alfalfa or the cloverleaf stand back then. The sun was shining. Was it shining then too? Who cares!

"Five minutes before the world was made ..."

I wanted to get going now, but hesitated and turned to the pilot. A shame had come over me, as though what I wanted to do must be done furtively and unobserved. I told him to pick me up in two hours. When I could no longer hear him, I set out on the way.

Before I knew it, when I turned around, the road had disappeared behind a gentle hill. Larks sang but it was otherwise still. I would've loved to sing. If something appropriate occurs to you, you must sing, I thought. I'd been walking quickly; now, however, unable to imagine anything more beautiful than walking here, I slowed down.

Time flew by. On and on the field before me stretched. I searched my mind for a simple melody, one whose notes I could hit and not screw up. An old Beatles song. Then a second and a third. I had an endless supply of them. By now I had gone much farther than Morler back then. Something in the distance stood out from the green of the fields. Most likely a farmhouse, and I suddenly thought of the two buildings I'd had burned to the ground. A number occurred to me. The number forty came to my mind. I'll go another forty paces.

ISBN: 978-3-96258-217-3

First Edition 2025

Original German Edition: *Fünf Minuten vor Erschaffung der Welt*
PalmArtPress, 2022

Cover Design: Catharine J. Nicely
Layout: NicelyMedia
Printed in Europe
In full accordance with the principles of sustainability,
this publication was printed climate-neutrally on FSC-certified paper.

PalmArtPress
Verlegerin Catharine J. Nicely
Pfalzburger Str. 69, 10719 Berlin
www.palmartpress.com

Selected Books from PalmArtPress

Martina J. Kohl
FAMILY MATTERS – *Of Life in Two Worlds*
ISBN: 978-3-96258-143-5
244 Pages, Novel, Softcover/Flaps, English

Kevin McAleer
L.A. KID
ISBN: 978-3-96258-193-0
316 Pages, Novel, Softcover/Flaps, English

Dennis McCort
The Golden Pot – *A Fairytale for Our Time*
ISBN: 978-3-96258-109-1
300 Pages, Softcover/Flaps, English

Patricia Paweletz
Tracing the Past in the Present – *En Route to Gaby Glückselig in New York*
ISBN: 978-3-96258-169-5
180 Pages, Non-Fiction, English

YoYo
One Man's Decision to Become a Tree
ISBN: 978-3-96258-136-7
268 Pages, Four Novellas, Softcover/Flaps, English

Rüdiger Görner
The Marble Song
ISBN: 978-3-96258-079-7
280 Pages, Softcover/Flaps, English

Sibylle Prinzessin v. Preussen, Friedrich Wilhelm Prinz v. Preussen
The King's Love – *Frederick the Great, His Gentle Dogs and Other Passions*
ISBN: 978-3-96258-047-6
Translation: Dennis McCort
160 Pages, Biography, Softcover/Flaps, English

Peter Wortsman
The Tattooed Man Tells All – *Der Tätowierte Mann*
ISBN: 978-3-96258-164-0
134 pages, Theater Play, Softcover/Flaps, English/German

Mitya New
Beyond Mount Kailash
ISBN: 978-3-96258-210-4
320Pages, NOVEL, English

Sophia Alexandra
Summer on the Subway
ISBN: 978-3-96258-152-7
118 Pages, Poetry, English

Carmen-Francesca Banciu
Fleeing Father
ISBN: 978-3-96258-083-4
152 Pages, English

Matéi Visniec
MIGRAAAAANTS! – *There's Too Many People on This Damn Boat*
ISBN: 978-3-96258-002-5
220 Pages, Theater Play, English/German

Michael Hampe
The Wilderness. The Soul. Nothingness – *About the Real Life*
ISBN: 978-3-96258-150-3
390 Pages, Phil. Novel, English

Reinhard Knodt
Pain – Schmerz
ISBN: 978-3-941524-77-4
200 Pages, Short Prose, Softcover/Flaps, English/German

John Berger
garden on my cheek
ISBN: 978-3-941524-77-4
Paintings by Liane Birnberg
60 Pages, Poetry/Art, Softcover/Flaps, English

Wolfsmehl
An Unsurpassed Age
ISBN: 978-3-96258-138-1
94 Pages, Theater Play, English

Wolf Christian Schröder was born in Bremen. He spent his childhood and youth in Kiel and Tübingen, later England. He then pursued a degree in Slavic Languages and Literature at the Free University of Berlin. He translated dramas from Russian and English. He wrote his own stage plays, receiving a commission from the Hamburg Schauspielhaus. Additional plays premiered in Hamburg, Hanover, Münster, Aachen, and Constance. He wrote the libretto for the musical "Die Liebe" at Ballhaus Ost, Berlin. His novel "Die Weissweintrinker" was published in 2020 by PalmArtPress, followed by his novel "Tapirgebein" in 2024. He received the Alfred Döblin Scholarship and a working scholarship from Künstlerhaus Villa Waldberta, Starnberger See.

Dennis McCort was born and raised in Hoboken, New Jersey, the 'mile square city' on the Hudson, in the shadow of Manhattan. He writes of his experiences growing up there in the postwar industrial era before gentrification in his memoir, "A Kafkaesque Memoir: Confessions from the Analytic Couch". McCort is now retired from Syracuse University where he taught German language and literature over a long career. He has authored scholarly books on Swiss writer C.F. Meyer and on the influence of Zen on such Western writers as J.D. Salinger, R.M. Rilke and Thomas Merton ("Going beyond the Pairs: The Coincidence of Opposites in German Romanticism, Zen and Deconstruction").